'Don't you want me?' Lucy asked.

David's eyes glittered with a hot intensity, but he said, 'I don't want to mess up your life.'

'It would only be a one-night stand.' She hesitated. 'We both know that's all this could be. I want to explore the passion you've unleashed. Please don't send me away.'

Suddenly he crossed the floor in two strides. The heat from his body, the scent of his flesh drugged her, assaulted her senses beyond enduring.

'I've wanted you from the moment I opened my eyes and saw you lying beside me,' he murmured, his husky voice edged with urgency.

He took her into his arms, and she melted, blindly seeking his lips. His mouth closed hungrily over hers—a hunger that matched her own.

He pulled away, breathless. 'Last chance. We should stop now.'

She pulled him back to her. 'No.'

When Debra McCarthy-Anderson and Carol Bruce-Thomas began writing romance novels as a team, they knew they'd need a pseudonym if there was to be any room left on the book cover! Thus the name **Debra Carroll** was born.

Friends since school, both writers make their homes in Toronto, but came to Canada from elsewhere—Carol from Newcastle, England and Debra from Calcutta, India. They explored divergent career paths before deciding to write fiction together. Debra's varied work in the entertainment field encompassed everything from concert production assistant to sound and light technician for a troupe of female impersonators. Meanwhile Carol became an analytical chemist, ran her own craft supply business and did some freelance non-fiction writing. Look for more books from this talented team!

DEBRA CARROLL is also the author of these novels in *Temptation®:*

ONE ENCHANTED NIGHT

BY

DEBRA CARROLL

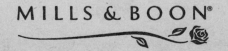

MILLS & BOON®

*All the characters in this book have no existence outside the imagination
of the author, and have no relation whatsoever to anyone bearing the
same name or names. They are not even distantly inspired by any
individual known or unknown to the author, and all the incidents are pure
invention.*

*First published in Great Britain 1998
by Harlequin Mills & Boon Limited,
Eton House, 18-24 Paradise Road, Richmond, Surrey TW9 1SR*

© Carol Bruce-Thomas and Debra McCarthy-Anderson 1997

ISBN 0 263 80884 X

21-9804

*Printed and bound in Great Britain
by Caledonian International Book Manufacturing Ltd, Glasgow*

Prologue

"DAMN!" HE HUDDLED down in his jacket against the biting wind, feeling a sharp stab of disappointment as he stared up at the darkened town house. Cheryl wasn't home yet.

He hadn't realized how much he'd counted on seeing her. He couldn't face the thought of going home to an empty house. Not tonight. The old place held too many memories of Mom and Dad—of happier times when he was young and blissfully ignorant of the world.

Cheryl made him feel so good. She kept the loneliness at bay. Right now his shoulders ached for the soothing touch of her fingers. He couldn't think of anything he wanted more than to fall asleep in her arms.

Unlatching the gate, he walked into the courtyard and up to the front door. Turning his back to the icy wind, he dug in his pocket for his keys. The snow hadn't started yet, but it was damn cold, even for January. He let himself in and quietly shut the front door. When he felt the instant warmth, his spirits revived. She was bound to be home soon.

Light from a streetlamp poured in through the long, narrow windows on either side of the door, showing him the way into the living room. The thick broadloom deadened his footsteps in the quiet house. Somewhere a clock ticked.

A thought hit him. Maybe she'd become tired of waiting for him, and was out attending to arrangements for the wedding. It should have been done weeks ago; the date was only a month off. But that was his fault. He'd been too busy with work. Cheryl hadn't complained, but somehow her stoicism only exacerbated his guilt. Well, he was back two days earlier than he'd expected. He would make it up to her.

He switched on the glass lamp on the end table and the room leaped into view—sleek and coolly modern; so different from the antique, book-strewn clutter of home.

He shrugged out of his parka, tossed it on the leather couch and sank down gratefully beside it. A whole day spent driving to Cornwall and back, on snowy, icy roads, had left him exhausted and aching, and in dire need of some tender loving care. The interview he'd pinned all his hopes on had fallen through. It had been a complete waste of time.

He could use a hot bath, preferably for two, with candles, soft music—the works. They could make slow, leisurely love among the bubbles. Then afterward, share some wine and dinner in front of the fire.

A fire. That was a good idea. He got up, took an artificial log from the holder on the hearth and put it on the grate. Setting a match to it, he sat back on his haunches, watching the flames take hold. Man-made logs were easy to get started but there was nothing like the smell of a real wood fire.

They would be enjoying one on the weekend. Maybe he could talk Cheryl into playing hooky tomorrow. They could get all the wedding stuff taken care of and then take off to the chalet a day early. A weekend of skiing up at Blue Mountain might help him shake off today's disappointment and decide what to do about his damn project. And if he didn't come any nearer to figuring that out, at least he would have Cheryl all to himself.

He stood, about to flop back onto the sofa again, when a muffled sound from above made him pause.

He listened intently for a moment, but heard only the crackle of the fire, loud in the silence around him. He shrugged, and was just lowering himself back down onto the couch when he heard it again. A dull thump.

His heart began to pound. Swiftly, noiselessly, he got to his feet, grabbed a poker from the fireplace and headed for the stairs, his adrenaline pumping.

He crept stealthily upward. Coming level with the second-floor landing, he stopped. Light glowed from under the bedroom door. Cheryl's room opened onto a balcony that overlooked the backyard. Someone could have gotten in that way.

His heart pounded harder against his ribs. Was he crazy? He'd seen enough death and destruction to know there was no percentage in being a hero. Maybe he should have called 911.

His mouth tightened into a grim line. By the time help arrived, it would have been too late.

Anyway, in the past he'd faced much worse than some punk thief. Tiptoeing cautiously down the hall, he paused outside the white door for a moment, listening.

A sound filtered through the wooden panels—a whispered voice. Then something that sounded like a moan in answer. There were two or more of them! Still, he had the element of surprise on his side.

Tightening his grip on the poker, he took a deep breath and counted silently to three. He raised the poker, flung open the door, and opened his mouth to yell. The sound choked in his throat as he stopped dead on the threshold.

Stunned, he just stood and stared. This had to be a nightmare.

In the soft lamplight, a naked couple lay slowly writhing in each other's arms on the bed. Cheryl, flushed with ecstasy, her blond hair tumbling over her shoulders, had her long legs wrapped around buttocks that fitted perfectly between her thighs.

The sheer eroticism of the scene shocked him. The breath left his body, as if he'd been kicked in the ribs.

Cheryl opened her eyes. Slowly, she focused on him. Passion fled, and her gaze sharpened in horror. "Oh, my God," she moaned. "No!"

Her partner turned his head, and he vaguely registered that it was Bill. His old buddy. Her old boss. Her very married old boss. But right now, that didn't matter. With a strange feeling of detachment, he watched Cheryl grab the sheet and pull it across her breasts. The irony of that gesture almost made him laugh.

There was nothing funny about this. And why was he still standing here?

"Excuse me. Please, don't get up."

Now *that* was a stupid thing to say. But suddenly he felt as if he were on the other side of a glass wall, watching a play in progress. His own voice sounded as if it had come from a million miles away. "I think three is definitely a crowd."

Backing out quickly, he shut the door and walked blindly down the hall. He'd just been fooling himself, he realized, thinking that he'd regained the ability to feel things like a normal person.

The door opened behind him and Cheryl rushed out. She caught up to him at the top of the stairs and clutched at his arm to stop him.

"Please, don't go yet! Let me explain." The desperation in her voice finally penetrated, and he felt a rush of sympathy for her obvious pain. Poor Cheryl. It really wasn't her fault.

"There's nothing to explain. I understand," he said as he started down the stairs.

"No, you don't understand." She still clung to his arm. "You have to listen."

"Okay, I'm listening." She didn't owe him any explanation, but for her sake, he paused halfway down the stairs and turned toward her.

She'd put on her blue terry bathrobe, one hand still clutching the lapels together protectively. For a moment she just stared up at him. Her beautiful face looked troubled—tormented even.

"Bill and I used to be lovers," she began slowly, the words husky and broken. "But I ended our affair when I started going out with you. Tonight... Tonight just happened. But it'll never happen again. You've got to believe me." Her voice sharpened with determination, and once again she reached out to clutch his arm as he resumed his walking and reached the bottom of the stairs.

"It's all right. I do believe you." The problem lay in him, not in what he'd seen tonight.

"What's the matter with you?" Anger darkened her

eyes and she tightened her fingers on his arm. "Any other man would be absolutely furious. But you! You're like a zombie."

Bingo! That was exactly what he was. "I just need to get away for a while and think."

Cheryl swiped furiously at her wet cheeks. "Think! What's there to think about? You just found me with another man. Don't you feel like…like, yelling, screaming, hitting somebody? Are you just going to walk away from this like some kind of coward?"

That word again. He felt a jolt of pain. Was that at the bottom of it all? Was he just a coward? "Would it serve any purpose if I hit somebody? I think we should talk about this when we're both calmer and more rational."

Cheryl said nothing, just bit her lip and looked away.

Distractedly, he looked around for his parka, then remembered he'd left it on the couch. Striding into the living room, he snatched it up and headed for the front door again.

Cheryl was standing where he'd left her, in the hall. "I do care about you, you must believe me…."

The fear in her eyes roused his sympathy again, and he said more gently, "I care about you, too. But we both need some time to think about what we're doing. I'm going skiing. We'll talk when I get back."

He yanked open the front door and lunged headlong into the frigid night air. The cold hardly penetrated the confusion churning inside him.

How deeply did he care for Cheryl? How deep did any of his feelings go?

His boots crunched on the thin layer of snow as he

walked quickly across the brick courtyard, his feet carrying him automatically down the quiet side street toward his car.

With Cheryl, it had seemed as though he'd made inroads on that numbing detachment he'd lived with for the past year. But anything he felt had only been superficial; it had taken this crisis to make him see it. Had his capacity to feel anything been destroyed forever?

He'd known all along that Cheryl wasn't in love with him. She wanted someone to take care of her, just as he needed someone to care for and think about so he wouldn't dwell on his own problems.

Had it been fair to Cheryl to bring his baggage into their marriage without telling her about his past, about what kind of man she would be marrying? He'd even lied to her about the bullet wound.

Reaching the Mercedes, he yanked open the door, tossed his jacket on the passenger seat and climbed in. When the engine purred to life, he put it in gear and headed off into the night. But as the city fell away behind him, he found he couldn't ignore the fear battering at him. And he couldn't block out her words, ringing in his ears...*some kind of coward.*

Was that at the root of it all? Had he blocked out every emotion because he was too afraid to face the truth?

1

"LUCY, ARE YOU READY? It's almost midnight!" Bea's impatient voice floated up the stairs to the attic studio.

"I'll be there in a minute," Lucy called back absently, bending over her illustration board to add another stroke to the rabbit's fur.

"Hurry, dear," Bea called again. "You know it won't take if we're even a second past midnight when we begin."

With a sigh, Lucy laid down her pencil and covered her tired eyes with her hands. "It won't take at all, because it's just a bunch of hocus-pocus," she muttered, torn between aggravation and amusement. Maybe her dear, sweet Great-aunt Bea had finally flipped her lid.

"Lucy!"

"Coming, coming." With one last, longing glance at the sketch, Lucy switched off the light above her worktable and stood.

She stretched and arched her back, working out the kinks from a long day at the drawing board. Through the small dormer window, all that could be seen was a whirling mass of snowflakes. Usually the lights of the Johnsons' farm—half a mile away—were clearly visible, but right now there was nothing out there but a white void. The wind moaned and rattled at the panes—a deliciously eerie sound. Snowflakes were already accumulating so thickly on the outer windowsill that the glass was becoming obscured.

"Lucy!"

Bea's sharp voice jerked her to attention. With another resigned sigh, Lucy went down to the second floor and paused at the top of the main staircase leading to the hall below.

Bea stood at the bottom, clutching the pineapple-carved newel post, an irascible frown on her small, wizened face. "Stop dithering and get down here. I have it all prepared."

Lucy expelled yet one more resigned breath. "I can't believe I've allowed you to talk me into doing this." She started walking down the broad, red-carpeted stairs. "This whole idea is completely insane."

"Oh, ye of little faith," Bea said, unmoved.

"Make that *no* faith. I don't believe in this nonsense. I'm humoring you, because you're probably getting a little senile. As soon as the weather improves, I'm taking you to Dr. Marshall and having you checked out." Reaching the bottom of the stairs, she gave her great-aunt a provocative grin.

Bea remained unfazed. "Don't you worry about my faculties. They're all there and working just fine."

"Mm-hmm. And this bizarre idea of yours only proves it," Lucy said teasingly. But she gave her great-aunt a hug and planted a kiss on her wrinkled forehead, inhaling the familiar fragrance of lavender. It was Bea's signature—that and the exotic aroma of her after-dinner hookah. Idiosyncrasies and crazy beliefs notwithstanding, Bea was still as sharp as a tack.

"I was driven to this 'bizarre idea' as a last resort, and you know it. In the past six months, since you broke up with Ethan—and I still don't understand that—I've had three perfectly nice young men over for tea, and you've found something wrong with every one of them. Mind you, I didn't blame you when it came to Dustin. Cute, but not too bright. Obviously you can't marry a stupid man."

"I'm glad you concede I'm not that desperate," she said dryly. "And as far as Ethan goes, we had to break up. We both knew from the start he'd be leaving town when his contract expired."

"You could have gone with him."

"I could have, if I'd loved him, but I didn't," Lucy countered lightly. They'd been over this before; she didn't need Bea to get started on that subject again.

"What was wrong with Doc Marshall's nephew, Ian?"

Too late. Here we go. "He was here on a holiday from Calgary," she patiently replied.

"Okay, but what's wrong with that nice Stewart boy? You went out with him a couple of times, then...nothing. I don't understand you, Lucy. He's handsome, smart, has a good job, lives in town. What more do you need in a husband?"

She felt a pang of dismay. There was no good answer for that one. What *was* wrong with Blaine? Nothing, but he didn't stir her in any particular way. And she wasn't going to think about marrying somebody unless she was in love.

The problem was, she had never even experienced love. Not that there had been that many men in her life, but there had been enough to choose from. Maybe she just wasn't capable of that particular emotion. Perhaps—and she hoped this wasn't the case—she wouldn't even know love when it came to her! Fortunately her great-aunt was too busy lecturing to notice her silence.

"You refuse to do anything about finding yourself a man. You just sit up there in that attic, day after day, lost in your own little world, while life passes you by—and I worry myself into old age." With an aggrieved sniff, Bea pulled a handkerchief from the pocket of her blue flowered dress, gave her dry eyes a wipe, and snuck a glance at Lucy to catch her reaction.

Lucy chuckled softly. "You old phony. If you're trying to make me feel guilty, it's not working."

Abandoning her hard-done-by demeanor, Bea shoved the handkerchief back into her pocket and gave Lucy a placid look. "Give me time, dear. I'm just warming up."

"Warm up all you like, but I won't marry Blaine just to make you happy. I like him, but he doesn't set the world on fire. What's the rush, anyway? I'm only twenty-seven."

"Exactly. In three more years you'll be thirty." Bea wagged her finger at her. "Your problem, Lucy, is that you read too much. World on fire, indeed. Now, come," she ordered imperiously.

Turning on her embroidered Turkish slippers, Bea marched quickly across the square entry hall toward the large living room that they usually kept for the paying guests. The back parlor was much cozier for just the two of them, especially in winter, but apparently it wasn't big enough for her great-aunt's purposes tonight.

At the open French doors, Bea stopped and turned,

her face alight with excitement and expectation. "Hurry, time's awasting."

An uneasy tremor went through Lucy as she slowly followed. Did Bea really believe in this stuff? It was one thing to humor her; it was another to allow her to delude herself.

She put a hand on her great-aunt's arm. It felt alarmingly thin—a sharp reminder that despite her energy, Bea was old and fragile. Lucy looked down into the faded blue eyes with concern and affection. "I hope you realize that this probably won't work. I don't want you to be too disappointed if nothing happens."

And of course, nothing *was* going to happen.

"Don't worry about me, my love. You don't get to be my age without learning a thing or two about coping with disappointment. I know that just asking for something doesn't mean one will get it. But is there any harm in trying?"

Once again, Lucy heaved a sigh of resignation. "No. No, of course not." There was no point in arguing, either. Turning to go into the living room, she stopped with a gasp.

While she'd been upstairs working, Bea had transformed the room. The furniture had been moved back to create a large space in front of the door. There, a six-foot-wide circle had been drawn in the center of the big old Persian rug with some kind of white powder. Within this circle lay a smaller one, made up of seven unlit black candles. More black candles burned on top of the bookshelves, along the windowsills and on the small tables scattered here and there beside the easy chairs and the old carved rocker. A crackling log fire burned in the grate at the other end of the room, and the rich, heavy scent of incense filled the air.

"You must wear this!"

Lucy turned her stunned gaze to Bea, who was holding out the most gaudy piece of clothing she'd ever seen: a voluminous cotton caftan, printed in a bilious paisley.

"Couldn't you have chosen something a little less garish? I mean, really—pink and yellow?"

"Rose and amber," Bea corrected impatiently. "For heaven's sake, child, I'm not asking you to parade down Main Street in it!"

"Oh...okay." Lucy gingerly took the robe from her great-aunt, wrinkling her nose in distaste. "But I still think this whole thing is silly. It's not even Halloween."

She slipped the robe over her head. Not only was it hideous; the thing was ten sizes too large. She held out her arms, looked down at it billowing around her, and giggled. "This evening Lucy is wearing a versatile creation by Omar the tent maker. You can lounge around in it, or it will sleep six...."

"Now, Lucy, you've got to take this seriously!" Bea chided. "This is no laughing matter."

"You could have fooled me," she muttered under her breath.

Ignoring her, her great-aunt continued, "And it won't work unless you concentrate on your desire."

"It's not *my* desire, it's *your* desire! Right now my only desire is to get back to my work and get it done."

"Work, work, work. That's all you ever think about! Right now we're concerned about the rest of your life."

"I'm perfectly content with my life, thank you. I like

my independence. I love my job. I'm very happy living here with you."

Bea wagged a small bony finger at her. "You can say that now, while you've got your youth and I'm still around, but wait till you're an old lady like me. I'll be dead, and you'll be alone. Loneliness is a terrible thing, Lucy."

"Okay, you're right, it's a terrible thing," she agreed hurriedly. She'd heard this spiel before. "But do you really think this is the way to remedy it?"

Bea sighed impatiently. "Blaine Stewart was your last hope for a man in this town, but you're not interested. I had no choice but to go to a higher power."

"I can't believe you don't see how ridiculous it all is!"

"You think this is ridiculous?" Bea's finely plucked and penciled brows rose sky-high. "I was sure you wouldn't care at all for the alternative."

"Which is?"

"A love potion."

Lucy grinned. "That doesn't sound so bad."

"Oh, doesn't it!" Bea shot her an arch look. "The ingredients include grated human skull and the froth from a pricked snail."

Lucy shuddered and held up her hand. "You're right. That sounds revolting. Even though I do think you're making it all up." She shook her head. "All right, let's get on with it, then."

With a triumphant smirk, Bea took her hand and led her to the circle.

Lucy poked at the marking on the carpet with the toe of her slipper. "What is this white stuff, anyway?"

"Just chalk."

"I hope this chalk vacuums up."

"Later." Bea waved her off impatiently as she took up a massive book that lay open on the coffee table and sank down into the old overstuffed velvet armchair; the huge, leather-bound volume dwarfed her tiny body. Bea picked up her tortoiseshell pince-nez and squinted down at the page. "Yes, here we are."

She looked up, and a glow of excitement added a tinge of pink to her thin cheeks. "Now, step into the circle and light the seven candles one by one in a clockwise direction. Use this." She handed her a burning candle from the table at her elbow.

Feeling like a complete idiot, Lucy took it, stepped into the circle and lit the candles one by one.

"Now, repeat after me..." Bea paused and consulted the book again. "Oh! You must recite these words as you walk around the candles while concentrating on your desire."

"Gotcha."

"'Oh, great Venus, we partition thee...'"

"Partition?" Lucy paused in midstep. "You mean, as in, divide into parts? I'm sure that'll impress the goddess."

"Cut the sarcasm, Lucy," Bea said shortly as once again she squinted down at the old book through the pince-nez. "No, that's petition. I'm afraid Great-grandmama was semiliterate. Her spelling is quite amazing. And her writing is awfully hard to read." She hefted the book onto the arm of the chair, tilted it toward the candle on the table beside her, and peered more closely at the page.

"More likely your prescription needs changing," Lucy said. "I told you, you need to get your eyes checked again. And I wish you'd use your proper glasses instead of those silly things."

"Yes, yes, later." Once again, her great-aunt waved her off with an impatient look. "Here, I suppose you'd better read it yourself—"

"Yeah, I'd better, or we'll be here all night."

Ignoring her words, Bea held the book toward Lucy with a worried frown. "If we get it wrong, there's no telling who, or what, we'll end up with."

Lucy took it from her shaky hands. "What do you mean, *who or what?* You mean I could end up with the Foul Fiend himself?"

"Please, Lucy, don't even joke about it!" With a shudder, Bea glanced around uneasily.

Lucy just chuckled and looked down at the book. The thing weighed about ten pounds and was hand-written on parchment in a faded brown copperplate that was difficult to decipher.

"Did this book really belong to your great-grandmother?"

"Yes. And when I die it will go to you. But we'll talk about that later. Come on, we don't have much time."

"Okay, but you keep an eye on the hem of this robe and make sure it doesn't catch on fire." With one hand Lucy tugged at the caftan and tried to stuff the excess fabric between her legs. Those candles on the floor were making her very nervous. "I don't want to go up in flames."

Bea gave her a withering look. "You young people these days, you have no sense of tradition! Now would you just read!"

Lucy looked down at the book again. "'Oh, Great Venus, we petition thee to fulfill thy daughter's desire.

Send her the fulfillment of her woman's pleasure. She is virgin, eternally unpenetrated.'''

Lucy bit back a laugh. If this was supposed to be her, it was stretching it a bit. "'Let her feel the power in her own orgasm.'" She stopped dead and looked over at her great-aunt, who smiled beneficently in approval. "You do realize that this is *completely* insane. This is never going to work."

"Shh." Bea put a finger to her lips. "Just keep reading."

"'In the name of the goddess, so be it done.'" Lucy looked up. "That's it?"

Bea nodded. "All except the dance. You do have the option of dancing around the circle as a way of winding things down."

"Dance? In this heat? I have neither the energy nor the inclination."

"Walk around the circle, then, just to be sure it takes."

Lucy rolled her eyes heavenward and plodded around the circle twice more. "*Now* can I step out?"

"Yes, dear."

Stepping over the chalk line, she handed the book back to Bea in relief. "See, nothing happened. Now, will you just forget all about this silly nonsense?"

Her great-aunt carefully laid the old book on the coffee table and shut it reverently. "Have some faith. These things take time. It could take a few hours, maybe even days."

"That's not the way it happens on 'Bewitched.' Samantha just wiggles her nose and poof, magic."

"Really, Lucy." Bea fixed her with a withering look. "This is real life, not television."

"Fine. Why don't you just call me when he gets here, then." Shrugging gratefully out of the voluminous robe, Lucy quickly folded it and handed it to Bea, feeling ten degrees cooler already. "I'll be upstairs."

Bea got up from her chair and followed her into the hall. "I'm not at all tired. How about some herbal tea?"

"No, thanks, you know I hate that stuff. But I won't say no to a real cup of tea." The grandfather clock in the corner began to chime. It was midnight.

Lucy had just reached the staircase when she heard a dull thud, like something heavy falling against the front door.

Pausing with one foot on the tread, she turned to Bea. "Did you hear that?"

Her great-aunt nodded, a little alarmed, but her blue eyes had a strange, expectant glitter. "I sure did."

Lucy cautiously approached the door. Rising on tiptoe, she peered through the small window. There was nothing out there but snow swirling around the porch, no sound but the howling wind and the slow chiming of the big old clock resounding through the house.

Sometimes birds flew at the windows, and with the same kind of sickening thud, knocked themselves out. But at night, and in this storm?

She slowly opened the door. Something big fell into the dimly-lit hallway to sprawl on the braided mat at her feet.

With a loud yelp, Lucy jumped back, gaping in astonishment at the inert figure. As the last stroke of midnight sounded, she heard Bea's excited cry.

"It's the magic! Why else would this have happened tonight? Lucy, your man is here!"

2

"DON'T BE RIDICULOUS, Bea."

Alarm made her speak more sharply than she'd intended. And yet... Had that crazy spell actually worked?

An icy gust of wind came through the open door, cutting through her sweatshirt and making her shiver. Sanity returned with a vengeance. "This man has obviously been in an accident."

"That doesn't mean he wasn't sent here to you," Bea said placidly, her conviction unassailable.

"For heaven's sake—" Lucy bit back her impatience. But this was no time to humor the quirks of old age. "He could be dying."

He wore no coat, only a heavy sweater over a shirt and jeans that were now thickly crusted with snow. His face and hair were matted not only with ice, but blood. He had some kind of wound on his forehead and he looked frighteningly pale. He could be dead already. A shiver of alarm raced through her.

Another blast of wind showered snow into the entrance hall.

"Here, let's get him in so we can close the door." Lucy sprang forward and grabbed his wrists. His flesh was icy, but he definitely wasn't dead...yet. She could feel a pulse, faint but steady.

But he was a deadweight. She pulled on his arms

and somehow managed to move him enough so that Bea could close the front door.

As it slammed shut on the howling wind, a sudden silence fell. Only the measured ticking of the clock filled the hall as Lucy stood and stared down at the stranger, her chest heaving from the exertion. "Why hasn't he woken up with all this rough handling?"

Bea sighed and shook her head. "I must say, I didn't expect him to arrive in this condition. The man's half-dead. You see, Lucy, you should have danced!"

Her mouth fell open as she looked at her great-aunt in disbelief. "Will you forget about the hocus-pocus for now? What are we going to do about him?"

Bea gave her an exasperated look. "Do? Why, thaw him out, of course."

"And then what? The roads are closed. We're here alone with a complete stranger who, for all we know, could turn out to be a guy named Jason with a thing for ice picks."

Bea stared at her as if she were mad. "What are you talking about?"

Lucy gritted her teeth. "He could turn out to be an escaped serial killer."

"With a face like this?" Bea knelt down and smoothed a snow-encrusted lock of honey brown hair off the man's broad and bloodied forehead. "Don't be ridiculous. He looks as gentle as an angel."

"May I remind you that Lucifer was an angel," Lucy said with heavy irony.

"And may I remind *you* that while we stand here arguing, this man could die from exposure? We need to warm him up."

"You're right." Lucy heaved a troubled sigh. Serial

killer or not, they couldn't let the man die. "The living room—it's stifling in there."

"Good thinking, dear."

"But how are we going to get him there? It was difficult enough moving him a few inches."

"I'll help you pull him in."

"With your back? Not a chance." Lucy chewed on her lip and looked down at the man lying on the mat in front of the door.

Tentatively, she put her hand on his shoulder. Another shiver of alarm trickled through her. Through the ice-encrusted sweater, her fingers curved over the swell of muscle on his upper arm. Ignoring the disturbing sensation in her fingertips, she shook him.

"Hey, mister..."

He didn't stir. She knelt beside him and shook him again a little harder, leaning closer to his face. "Wake up. Come on, please, wake up...."

Suddenly his arm came up to wrap around her shoulders and he pulled her down onto him. His hold was surprisingly strong, and she found herself plastered against a hard chest. She caught her breath. Her face was mere inches from his. Then his eyes opened. They were bright blue, and scowling at her.

"Who are you?" His voice was low and rusty.

"I'm Lucy Weston," she gasped out, still locked tightly against him.

But she hardly noticed his irritability, and barely heard Bea's surprised squeak. All her concentration was focused on the burning, tingling sensation along her body where it was pressed against his. So familiar. A perfect fit. Like Cinderella's slipper.

The next moment she snapped back to her senses.

Cinderella's slipper? The cold wind must have frozen a few of her brain cells.

She struggled against his hold, but she needn't have worried. His arm went slack and fell to his side. His eyelids fluttered shut. It looked as if he'd passed out again.

Quickly she hoisted herself off him, trying to ignore the trembling in every nerve ending. She was tired and freaked out; that was why she was behaving so strangely. But right now she had to get a grip on herself and figure out what to do.

An idea occurred to her; one she would have thought of sooner if her brain were functioning normally.

"I'll get him into the living room," she told Bea decisively. "You get some bedding and make up the couch. Get lots of warm blankets."

"Right!" Brisk and businesslike, Bea nodded and hurried away up the stairs.

"Don't die, please don't die," Lucy muttered breathlessly, and grabbed the edges of the rug beside his shoulders. Slowly, with painful effort, she dragged the laden carpet across the polished wooden floor. "And please don't turn out to be a serial killer."

She stopped abruptly. A trickle of alarm raced through her as she realized her fervent wish had nothing to do with concern for their safety. Was she mad?

Better to forget that weird sensation. She began tugging at her load again, her arms starting to ache from the effort. She pulled her burden over the threshold into the living room, where the thick carpet slowed her down even further. Now her back hurt, too, but she tried to ignore it.

It seemed to take forever to drag him to the warmth of the hearth, and she was sweating freely by the time she hauled him alongside the sofa near the fireplace.

Bea rushed in, half hidden by the stack of bedding clutched in her arms. "I got every spare quilt I could find," she said breathlessly as she dropped her load on the floor. The two of them hurriedly made up a bed on the big old red velvet couch.

"There, that should be plenty warm." Bea spread a fourth quilt—a faded rose of Sharon—on top of the cozy pile, and smoothed it in place. "Now, let's get him out of these wet clothes. Help me."

Bea knelt down and began untying the laces of one hiking boot. After a moment's hesitation, Lucy crouched beside her and began to work on the other. It seemed to take ages to get the frozen, knotted laces undone. Her fingers were cold and aching by the time they finally got his boots and socks off.

"The sweater next," Bea said, all bustling authority.

Disturbed, Lucy hesitated. There was something illicit about undressing an unconscious man. It seemed like such an invasion of privacy. But did they have much choice?

The snow covering him had begun to melt, soaking his clothes. From what little she knew about hypothermia, getting him warm and dry was the first priority. But that was easier said than done.

He was a deadweight and it was a struggle to remove his Aran-knit sweater, but finally they managed. Now for the faded denim shirt. With trembling fingers, Lucy began undoing the small buttons.

With each button, a little more of his chest was revealed. And with each button, her pulse raced a little faster.

She tried not to notice how smoothly his skin stretched over the muscles of his torso, with just a sprinkling of hair between the brown nipples.

Catching her breath, she averted her gaze. But as she slid off the shirt, she saw a patch of ugly scar tissue near his left shoulder, just above the heart. What on earth could have caused such a terrible wound?

"Help me with his jeans, Lucy." Bea's peremptory order put an end to her uneasy speculation, but it gave her something else to worry about.

No, not the jeans! She just couldn't.

But there was no way around it; he would have to get out of his clothes. Resolutely, she unzipped his fly, clenching her teeth as her knuckles brushed against the bulge under the fabric. What was the matter with her? So he had an attractive body. So what? But her mouth went uncomfortably dry as she and Bea pulled the sodden denim down over his hips and yanked the jeans off.

He now lay stretched out on the rug, wearing only a pair of white briefs that had slid very low on his hips. Lean, masculine hips. The briefs were soaking wet, too, and clung to him in a way that left little to the imagination. And "little" didn't exactly describe it, either.

"They've got to come off, as well," Bea said briskly. "Give me a hand, Lucy."

As her cheeks flamed, she averted her gaze and slipped her fingers under the elastic waistband. With Bea's help, she peeled off the underwear.

"Oh, my..."

At her great-aunt's breathless sigh, she couldn't help peeking.

Oh, my. She swallowed hard. Not too big, just perfectly shaped and proportioned. Speaking purely from an artistic point of view, of course.

"Bea, we shouldn't," she admonished faintly. "This is taking advantage in the worst way—looking at someone's body when they're out cold."

"For goodness' sake, don't be such a prude, child." Bea's rapt gaze ran over his long, naked limbs. "The human body is a beautiful thing and there's no harm in admiring it. And he's *such* a fine specimen."

"If we don't get this 'fine specimen' under some covers soon, he'll be a dead one," Lucy replied, a little too desperately. The truth was, if they didn't cover him up soon, *she* would be the one in trouble. The intensity of her reaction to this man amazed her more than a little.

They'd found no wallet in any of his pockets, no identification at all. Somehow that made it worse. She had no business ogling a nameless stranger.

"Let's get him up on the couch," she said briskly.

Taking care to keep her gaze scrupulously above his waist, she stood over him, took hold of his ice-cold hands, then pulled him to a sitting position.

"Get behind him, quick," she panted to Bea. "And hold him up."

Bea knelt behind him, putting her hands on his shoulders and pushing him forward. His head lolled onto his chest. "Now what?"

"I'm going to try and get the top half of him onto the couch first, then the bottom."

Still being careful to keep her gaze averted, she

planted her feet on either side of his hips, bent her knees and looped her arms under his.

Although she was determined not to get too close, somehow her face ended up pressed against the column of his neck. She could smell a wonderfully masculine scent—his soap or cologne, probably. Doing her best to ignore it, she braced herself and tried to lift, straining every muscle.

She managed to raise his arms above his head, but the rest of him stayed put. Exasperated, she blew her bangs off her forehead and glared at his inert form. This wasn't going to work!

Like it or not, she would have to put her body into it, although that meant getting too close for comfort. But she consoled herself with the thought that the sooner she got him on the couch, the sooner she could cover him up.

Wrapping her arms more firmly around him, she prepared to lift, but that only brought her chest up against his. With a sharp, tingling jolt, her nipples tightened into hard, unbearably sensitive little buds. The shock almost made her drop him.

At this rate, she would never get him onto the couch. And surely there was something warped about responding like that to a man who was out cold and felt like a block of ice.

Gritting her teeth, she tried to ignore her depraved reaction and thanked God he wasn't awake to feel it. Now *that* would be embarrassing.

Taking a deep breath, she heaved with all her might. He still didn't budge. She tried again, straining and grunting until finally her legs buckled. Laying him on the carpet, she stood and stared down at him. She was panting for breath as if she'd just run a marathon.

Wiping the sweat off her forehead with the back of her hand, she tried to calm her racing heartbeat. Who was this man? And why did he have this strange effect on her? A surge of anger made her grit her teeth. Why did he have to compound the problem by being so damn helpless?

"This won't work. It's impossible," she said in frustration. "He's just going to have to stay on the floor."

"I'm afraid you're right," Bea agreed, and immediately began hauling the bedding off the couch.

Quickly, they rearranged the quilts on the carpet in front of the couch, using two beneath him for a mattress. They rolled him onto the makeshift bed and Lucy covered him up with profound relief.

While she tucked the other quilts in around him, Bea left the room, and returned a few moments later with a bowl of water, a facecloth, and the first-aid kit. She set both down on the carpet beside Lucy.

"I'm going to call Doc Marshall. You clean him up." She bent down and picked up the bundle of his wet clothes. "I'll toss these in the laundry. He won't be needing them for a while."

As the tiny figure bustled out of the room, Lucy eyed their guest nervously. He was breathing so lightly it was difficult to tell if he was breathing at all. She knew he needed tending, but she felt oddly panicked at the thought of having to touch him some more.

She could hear Bea's voice in the hall; she was already talking to the doctor. After a moment she bustled into the room, checked the man's pupils and went back to the phone.

Wetting the facecloth, Lucy began to gingerly sponge off the dried blood from his face. Bea was right about his looks. Slowly she cleaned him up, admiring his well-molded lips, his straight, attractive nose and the contours of his strong masculine jaw.

The thick, honey brown hair springing back from his forehead was on the long side and slightly wavy. Delicately, she dabbed at the darkly crusted blood around his hairline and found to her relief that there was only a small bump there, and a gash that had already stopped bleeding. Even so, she dressed it with some gauze.

"He looks a lot better," Bea said with approval as she came bustling back into the living room. "Oh, isn't he handsome! Lucy, you're so lucky!"

"Bea, please, stop it," she begged. "You know very well this has nothing to do with that silly spell. I'm worried—he's still unconscious. What did Dr. Marshall say?"

"That it's probably a concussion," Bea said matter-of-factly. "We'll have to nurse him till the weather breaks."

That was not what Lucy wanted to hear. "But we know nothing about nursing. We haven't a clue...." Her voice rose to a panicky pitch.

"We'll be fine and so will he," Bea declared placidly.

"Why did he have to come here?" she demanded bitterly. "Why couldn't he have gone to someone capable of looking after him? What if he dies because we don't know what we're doing?"

"He didn't come here. He was sent here. We're quite capable of looking after him and he's not going to die," Bea stated firmly. "What's the matter with you? You didn't get into a panic like this when you hauled Abe Johnson down to the hospital that day he was fool enough to get his hand caught in the harvester.''

That was different. The prompt explanation that sprang into her mind startled and disturbed her. The truth was, Mr. Johnson didn't have this disconcerting effect on her.

She wrenched her attention back to Bea.

"Now, I was given detailed instructions. We have to keep him in a darkened room, so put out all those candles.''

Lucy shot to her feet, glad to be doing something, and went around the room blowing the candles out.

Bea poked at the glowing logs in the hearth and set the fire screen back in place. "The fire's pretty low now. I don't think we need to worry about that. Besides, it's important to keep him warm. But we've got to raise his head and shoulders and turn him on his side." She knelt down next to him. "Here, give me a hand.''

Reluctantly, Lucy joined Bea and helped her adjust the man's position, stuffing another cushion under his head. That done, she sat back on her heels and stared at him.

"Now we must try to rouse him every hour," Bea directed her as she got to her feet. "Which means we're going to have to sit up with him all night. I'll go put on a pot of coffee—''

"No," Lucy interrupted. "You'll go to bed.''

The hall clock had just struck one, and she'd noticed that her great-aunt was looking a little drawn. "There's no reason for us both to stay up. I'll take the first shift.''

"But I should be here to help you! What if he wakes up?"

She shook her head. "If he's going to need around-the-clock nursing till we can get him to a hospital, we'll have to take turns. You can take the morning shift."

Bea opened her mouth to argue and Lucy hurriedly continued. "You're not going to dispute the cosmic order, are you? You've always said that I'm the night owl, and you're the lark that rises with the new day, remember?"

Bea's lips compressed in annoyance and Lucy smothered a triumphant grin. Every once in a while—but not often enough—she caught her great-aunt and hoisted her on her own petard.

Enjoying the moment, she drove the point home. "You keep telling me that we function best when we're in harmony with our natural rhythms, or something like that. And you *know* I work best at night."

As Bea went reluctantly up the stairs, Lucy closed the beveled-glass French doors, to keep in the heat. She walked softly through the big, dark room over to the old velvet armchair nestled in the curve of the big bay window.

Taking the crocheted purple afghan off the back of the chair, she wrapped it around herself and settled in to keep watch over her patient. Sitting in the shadows, she was as far from the man as the room would allow.

Outside, the fury of the wind had died down, hardly any sound of it penetrating now through the heavy velvet curtains. Suddenly she became aware of how quiet it was.

Then she heard the faint ticking of the clock in the hall, and the subdued crackle and hiss of the low fire.

The only light came from the dull glow of the slow burning logs in the grate.

Leaning her head back against the soft upholstery, she stared at the stranger. His face was in shadow; the firelight behind him glowed on his hair like a halo.

This was too unreal. Had it only been a few hours ago that she'd been upstairs, quietly doing her work and minding her own business? And then, bang, out of the blue...

But had it come out of the blue?

She shifted restlessly in the chair. This man landing on their doorstep was sheer coincidence, nothing more. He most definitely wasn't the result of magic, whatever Bea might want to believe. But perhaps it was possible that the spell had somehow subliminally influenced her. She'd never experienced such a strong sexual reaction.

There had to be a logical reason why. Did it have something to do with all those charged ions out there in the storm? Maybe that, and her own tiredness, accounted for the overreaction to him. She glanced at her watch to see that it was only one-thirty. At this hour she was usually wide-awake; she hardly ever went to bed before three. But tonight, of all nights, she felt inexplicably sleepy.

A moan pierced the silence, bringing her abruptly back from her disturbing reflections. The quilts covering her patient were trembling, and even from where she sat she could hear his teeth chattering.

She quickly untangled herself from the afghan and hurried across the room, sinking down to her knees at his side. Her heart hammered painfully in her chest as she stared at him uncertainly.

What was the matter with him? He was shivering violently. How could he possibly be cold under that mountain of quilts? Tentatively, she tucked the covers around him more closely, but the shivering increased and he began muttering, his voice low and unintelligible.

Alarmed, she reached under the covers, and met his hand. It was ice-cold. A knife edge of panic ran down her spine, but she deliberately suppressed it. This was no time to get into a flap; she had to use her common sense.

The doctor had stressed the importance of keeping him warm, and there wasn't another blanket in the house.

Without giving herself time to think, she slipped under the covers and curled herself along his back, putting her arm around him. Immediately, his arm covered hers and his hand curled over her fingers, clutching them tightly. To her utter amazement, his body relaxed heavily into the curve of hers.

At the contact, a burning jolt of electricity shot through her, so frighteningly intense she would have jumped right back out again, except that his shivering had immediately begun to subside and his body stilled. That was good; she'd been afraid the violent shuddering could aggravate his head injury.

He gave a sigh, and she felt him relax and snuggle even closer, molding himself against her as if it were the most natural thing in the world.

But as his naked body nestled into hers, with his backside curving into her hips, a moist heat began to uncurl low in her belly.

Oh, no. She held her breath, trying to stifle the inexplicable, unbelievable flood of sensation. Every inch of her skin seemed to tingle, her breasts felt swollen and sensitive, and between her thighs the little pulsing waves of pleasure became stronger and stronger. This couldn't be what it seemed to be. She was actually hovering on the brink of... If he moved even a fraction...

With another sigh, he relaxed even more. His firm buttocks pressed against her, and suddenly everything exploded.

She shuddered helplessly, as wave upon wave of sensation surged through her. She shouldn't be allowing herself to feel this! It was all wrong, depraved. But she couldn't stop the overwhelming flood of release until the last aftershock died away and finally she lay beside him, exhausted and stunned.

She tried to pull away, but his hand tightened on hers, preventing her from moving. Alarm shot through her. Was he awake, aware of what had just happened to her? She raised her head and looked down at his face. His eyes were shut; he was obviously in a deep sleep.

Only a little reassured, she slowly laid her head back down on the pillow.

What had just happened? That was a stupid question. She knew damn well what had happened. But how? Who was this man, that he could do this to her?

His shivering had ceased altogether now and he was quiet, molded so naturally close. Amazingly enough, in spite of what had just occurred, her urge to escape had vanished. She wanted to lie here and hold a total stranger in her arms because it felt good—and there was *nothing* natural about that. Perhaps she was dreaming.

But no, this was no dream. This was much too real. There was nothing imaginary about the hard body pressed against hers, relaxed completely now. His breathing was deep and even. Somehow she knew that he was finally sleeping, and not unconscious.

And now that he was safely asleep, she should really get up. But it felt so warm and comfortable under the covers. A warning flashed through her head that she mustn't get *too* comfortable.

SQUEEZED UPSIDE DOWN in a dark, cramped box, somehow he righted himself and crawled toward the small patch of dim light.

A gust of howling wind pelted his face with stinging snow and snatched away his breath until he knew he would suffocate.

He staggered to his feet and began to walk. Needles of fiery cold turned his flesh to ice. All he could do was keep going, get away from something that hurt unbearably. What was it?

But he couldn't get away from the pain. It throbbed and pounded in his head, making him sick and dizzy. He couldn't remember ever feeling so miserable. His legs kept moving under him, numb and automatic; he couldn't even feel them anymore.

He stumbled on, walking until time had no meaning. Was he going to freeze to death? At least then, the pain would stop—the terrible red-hot pain that slammed and hammered around his skull with every footstep.

All around him was a white, freezing void. Then, dim and far away, a yellow glow. He had to reach the light, and warmth. Would he ever feel warm again?

A soft voice echoed. Must be a dream. Or maybe he

was dead; hearing the voices of angels. But no, dead men felt no pain, and the pain was still there, splitting open his skull.

Struggling up through a terrible white blankness, he fought to open his eyes. So heavy, so heavy. Panic rose inside. If he didn't open his eyes he would drown in smothering mists.

Wake up! A moan filled his ears, and he knew it was his own voice. Slowly, his eyes opened, but at first it was all a blur. The light was pain. The orange glow resolved itself into flickers of brightness reflecting off the prisms of a small chandelier far above where he lay.

He could feel the warmth behind his head, and knew it was a fire. Heat. God, it felt so good. If he was dead, then death wasn't so awful.

And this must be...Heaven? It looked too pleasant to be hell—this high-ceilinged, old-fashioned room, with a dark, overstuffed couch looming above him, and the gleam of polished wood where the carpet ended.

Was he still dreaming? Couldn't be. His head hurt too much. The pain was real enough.

Something warm nestled behind him, warm and soft and quietly breathing. He turned his head, and arrows of fire shot through his skull, while the room spun dizzily. He closed his eyes and fought down the rising nausea.

Slowly the dizziness began to subside, but the pain kept up the relentless pounding. He opened his eyes again, and very slowly turned his head.

He froze and held his breath, forgetting the pain for a moment. Now he knew he was dreaming.

A woman curved close to his side, fast asleep. Her dark hair was tousled around a face too lovely to be real. A thick sweep of lashes brushed against her smooth cheeks, and her rosy lips were full and soft and moist. Her breath felt warm against his throat. Her arm curved around his waist; her fingers were soft on his skin.

A shock of awareness rushed through him: He was naked.

LUCY WOKE WITH A START, becoming instantly aware of the bare male chest under her arm, the naked shoulder under her chin. She hadn't meant to drop off to sleep. What on earth was the time?

Carefully, she lifted her arm off his chest and peered at her watch. Six-thirty! She was supposed to have roused her patient once every hour.

Raising her head to peer into his face, she met the stranger's bright blue eyes, staring at her.

A rush of heat washed through her. Quickly removing her arm, she slipped out from under the covers in one hurried movement.

The cool air made her shiver, and she felt disoriented. Although he made no effort to move, or speak, there was something unsettling in the direct expression of his intensely blue eyes—something that seemed to reach right down inside her, and made her afraid that he could see her shameful secret: her unnatural, illicit response to him—a complete stranger.

"You couldn't get warm, you see. It was the only thing I could think of." She cleared her throat. Her voice was thick and her tone defensive. Self-consciously, she tugged at her rumpled sweatshirt as the stranger continued to stare at her. "I didn't mean to fall asleep beside you...."

"Where am I?" His voice finally emerged, a husky croak. He slowly licked his dry lips. "How did I get here?"

"I guess you walked. Don't you remember?"

"I remember being cold," he said slowly.

"That's not surprising," she added quickly. "You had no coat on. What happened to you? Were you in an accident?"

"I guess so...." He put a hand to his forehead, touched the gauze dressing and winced. "My head hurts like hell."

"You cut it. Do you remember how?"

He slowly shook his head, then winced again and closed his eyes. After a few moments he opened them to stare at her. "Where am I?"

"You're in Hazeldene. We're halfway between Orangeville and Collingwood. Were you in a car accident? Where were you heading?"

He didn't answer her questions, just kept his intent gaze fixed on her. "Who are you?"

"I'm Lucy Weston. I told you before, don't you remember?"

"Did you take my clothes off?"

"My Great-aunt Bea and I did, yes." The heat surged back into her cheeks.

Unable to look at him, she walked a few paces and knelt down by the fireplace. Throwing on another log, she stoked the embers until flames began to lick around the wood.

"We had to. They were soaking wet and we were afraid you'd die of hypothermia...." She trailed off, feeling acutely embarrassed.

He didn't respond, and she snuck a look at him. A

small frown creased his brow. What was he thinking, and why did she care? But suddenly she felt very vulnerable.

She moved away from the fire and stood over him. "Who are you?" Her words came out sharply, and she was suddenly aware that her defensiveness was showing. But she couldn't help herself. Questions tumbled out. "What's your name? Where do you come from? You had no identification on you. You weren't even wearing a coat."

The bright blue eyes held hers for a long moment, then he said slowly, "I don't know. I don't remember."

"What do you mean?" Foreboding crept in, making her stomach muscles tighten.

"I mean, I don't remember anything. Where I came from, what happened to me." He paused, and his eyes filled with alarm. "I don't even know who I am."

3

"OF COURSE, YOU DON'T!" The brisk voice startled him, and suddenly, out of the gloom, a wizened little figure came hurrying toward him. "I mean, it would be quite remarkable if you did, wouldn't it?"

The darkened room reeled sickeningly around him, and he closed his eyes. He had the awful feeling of being lost in a huge, black void. No matter how he struggled, he couldn't remember anything about himself. And nothing made sense anymore.

Maybe he'd been given some kind of drug and he was hallucinating. At least he hoped it was a hallucination. The alternative was too frightening. If he could just get back to sleep, with any luck he would wake up to reality.

But the rustle of fabric made him open his eyes again. Wrapped in a bright red satin housecoat, the old woman had sunk down on the carpet beside him. From beneath a dizzying print scarf, tied around her head Aunt Jemima-style, a pair of bright eyes peered at him intently.

"We conjured you up from the void, you know."

"Bea!" The word exploded into the quiet room.

He turned his head, only to feel a blinding shaft of pain and another sickening wave of dizziness. He shut his eyes and waited for the whirling to subside.

No more quick moves.

"Bea, please, not now," the younger one said more calmly, but he could still hear the tension underlying her words.

Slowly, he opened his eyes. The blurry outlines of the room came into view and sharpened as his vision gradually cleared.

The young woman—Lucy—stood above him, her hands clenched tightly into fists at her sides. Even in the orange light of the fire, he could see her cheeks glowing with embarrassment and her green eyes blazing with resentment as she glared at the old lady.

But the old lady paid no attention. "I do beg your pardon, I haven't even introduced myself! I'm Bea Weston. You've already met Lucy. She's my grand-niece, you know, but we don't bother with the 'grand' part. That can be so tedious. Now you can just call me Bea, like Lucy does."

As she prattled on, she was busy looking him over very carefully, with an approving smile on her lips that made him a little uneasy. Who was this woman? And what was wrong with her?

"Now of course, you don't have a name. Yet. That's the first thing we'll have to remedy. And naturally it will have to be the right name. Not just *any* name will do."

He stared up at the apparition, looming over him in the firelight, and felt as if his head were turning inside out. If this was a dream, then it was one for the books.

"Bea. Please, not now," Lucy repeated meaningfully. "This man has amnesia. He can't remember anything."

"I know what amnesia is, Lucy," the old lady admonished haughtily. "And you can believe what you want to, but this just reaffirms the wisdom and goodness of the goddess. Not only does she supply the man, but she sends one with a blank slate. Such perfection.'' She ended with a euphoric sigh.

After this bewildering speech, silence filled the room. The old woman continued to gaze down at him, a satisfied smile on her thin lips. Carefully, he shifted his gaze to her niece.

The flush on her smooth cheeks had deepened. Under her loose green sweatshirt, her small, slender chest rose and fell rapidly. She wasn't looking at him—she was glaring at her great-aunt—but the old lady seemed blithely unaware.

Then, suddenly, Lucy turned her gaze on him. Her green eyes, framed by thick, dark lashes, seemed to glow with an eerie light. But right now the mysterious eyes were filled with acute mortification. It was obvious that she was intensely embarrassed.

A burst of compassion took him by surprise. He wanted to reach out and take her hand, reassure her—until he realized that if it weren't for him being here, there would be no problem.

''Listen...'' He swallowed and licked his dry lips. The words still didn't come out easily from his burning throat. ''I really appreciate you taking me in, but I'm fine now, so if somebody will just get me my clothes, I'll be out of here.''

''Absolutely not!'' Bea rapped out adamantly. ''You're in no condition to leave.''

''But I can't impose on you any longer,'' he said, equally firmly, and meant it.

It was bad enough not knowing anything, but he

couldn't stand the feeling—growing stronger by the minute—that he was a major nuisance.

Except he couldn't for the life of him figure out how he would manage walking out of here. He couldn't even turn his head without feeling as if he was going to black out. But get out, he must.

"Believe me, my dear, you're not imposing. You're doing us a favor. Besides, the spell doesn't say anything about you leaving."

Spell? What was she talking about?

"I'm not sure I understand," he began uncertainly, then paused. What was there to understand? After all, insanity was incomprehensible, wasn't it?

"Lucy, explain it to him." The old lady still smiled down at him placidly.

He heard Lucy's sharp, indrawn breath and saw her glaring daggers at her great-aunt. Then she turned—reluctantly, he thought—to look directly at him. Behind her grim expression, there was more than a hint of self-conscious embarrassment.

"You may as well know the truth," she said stiffly. "You're most likely suffering from a concussion. We're snowed in, maybe for another day, perhaps more. And I'm no nurse. But we've been on the phone to the doctor and he's given us instructions on what to do for you."

"*That's* not what I wanted you to explain," Bea piped up. "Tell him about the spell."

"The spell?" he asked. "What spell?"

"The one we performed to summon you, of course," Bea chirped. "How do you think you got here?"

The throbbing in his head intensified, and he squeezed his eyes shut for a moment. There was no maybe about it anymore. The woman was a genuine fruitcake. But—and he wasn't sure he was strong enough to hear the answer right now—how did he get here?

"Why don't we wait till he's feeling a little better before we bombard him with too much information." From her mollifying tone he could tell Lucy was humoring the old lady.

"You're right, dear. We certainly don't want to overwhelm him," Bea replied, thoughtfully nodding her head in agreement.

Too late. He was about as overwhelmed as a person could get.

Then Lucy turned to him and, despite her obvious tension, gave him a look of entreaty that tacitly begged his understanding for her strange old great-aunt.

Adrift as he was in this fantastic world, her silent entreaty suddenly grounded him in reality. It touched a core of compassion in him. And yet at the same time, he felt uneasy at the depth of feeling it stirred. He didn't even know her.

"Don't worry about a thing, my dear." The old lady beamed down at him placidly, but in the orange glow of the fire, her small, wrinkled face looked almost demonic. "We'll take good care of you."

The uneasy feeling deepened. Whether or not this was a dream, he sensed danger here. He didn't understand it, and he didn't want to try; his head hurt too much to think. He just wanted to get out.

But he had to face it: He was stuck here, weak as a baby, at the mercy of these strangers—one of whom was most likely crazy.

"I'm going to call the doctor again." Lucy cut into his thoughts.

"You go right ahead." The old lady suddenly leaped to her feet so energetically, he was taken aback. "*I'm* going to find him a name!" An excited glow spread over her small, pointed face, making her look more like a pixie than ever. "Now where did I put that book of names? Oh, yes, I remember now."

She smacked her hands and did a strange little jig before sashaying out of the room, humming tunelessly. He could only stare after her. Had that little creature really been here, or had he strayed into a fantasy world?

Words came into his head, unbidden. "'Twas brillig, and the slithy toves/Did gyre and gimble in the wabe...''

Lucy had gotten as far as the door. She stopped abruptly to spin around and stare at him. "What did you say?" Her sharp voice penetrated the daze.

"Nothing... I..."

He shook his head in an attempt to clear the fog from his brain, then immediately wished he hadn't. The hammers slammed into his skull again. He winced and shut his eyes as once again the room swung sickeningly around him.

When he opened his eyes, Lucy stood over him, a slight frown on her pale brow, uncertainty in her eyes.

"You just quoted from *Through the Looking Glass.*" Her voice was tense. "You must remember something, then."

"Lewis Carroll... Yes..." He searched his mind for more, but only came up with smothering darkness. "I suppose I must have read the book, but I don't remember."

"Yet you know the author," she said quickly. "Can we assume you're a man who likes to read?"

"Can we? I can't assume anything. I can't even rule out your great-aunt's theory about my being plucked from the void. Although I feel more like I've landed in it."

"I don't doubt it," she said stiffly. "But I hope you don't take any of that seriously."

A fleeting look of...panic? filled her eyes, but then it was gone. He must have imagined it, along with everything else. He licked his dry lips, suddenly realizing how terribly thirsty he was.

"Could I have some water, please?" People could get thirsty in their dreams, too. At least, he hoped so.

"Water... Yes, of course, how silly of me." Her voice held unmistakable relief. "I'll get some right away."

He was barely aware of her hurrying out of the room as a picture burst into his mind, sudden and vivid: parched brown earth and a cluster of mud huts; the relentless sun, burning down from a brassy sky; half-naked kids crouching at a muddy stream.

WHEN LUCY CAME BACK into the living room with a jug of water and a glass on a tray, she found Bea perched on the couch, her feet tucked under her.

She sat leafing through another of her old books, a small one this time, with yellowing pages that were coming away from the crumbling green binding.

"Now, let's see. How about Doyle? Do you like that one? It's a Celtic name meaning dark stranger. Although, you're not really dark, are you?"

She peered down at the man, who was staring at her as if she were about to spring horns. And who could blame him? This must all seem like a nightmare.

Lucy put the tray down on the side table and poured a glass of water. To her chagrin, her hands shook slightly.

"Let's see... Ah! Dorian. Now that means a gift. And that's what you are."

"A gift?" he said dubiously.

"Yes, from the gods." Her tone implied that it should be perfectly obvious. "Don't like that one?" Bea asked, unfazed. "Not to worry." She went back to scanning her book.

The room had been growing steadily brighter as weak daylight crept around the curtains—enough for Lucy to see the mixture of wariness and bemusement in his vivid blue eyes. It was as if he couldn't decide whether to burst out laughing or take to his heels.

Either way, he wasn't strong enough to cope with this, and neither was she. She handed him the glass of water and interjected, "Bea, perhaps you could call Dr. Marshall and let him know how our patient is doing this morning."

"In a minute, Lucy." Bea ignored her, continuing to flip the loose pages of her book. "Saul? No, that wouldn't suit you at all. Although it does mean desired. And goodness knows, we've desired you long enough, haven't we, Lucy?"

His gaze slid over to her. She could barely meet it, much less act nonchalant. Not because of Bea's outrageous remarks, but because of her own guilty secret.

While this man slept, innocent and trusting, she'd had her way with him. Maybe it had been totally unanticipated, but there was still something utterly debauched about it. Especially since it had been the best sexual experience she'd ever had.

God forbid he should ever guess where desire had led her.

"Hmm..." Bea was still murmuring to herself. "Charles, perhaps? 'Strong and manly' seems an apt description." Her eyes twinkled down at him, then darted back to the book. "Let's see, Damon... David..."

"David?" His voice sharpened.

"Oh, do you like that one?" Bea perked to attention.

"Does it sound familiar?" Lucy added hopefully.

He was frowning, deep in thought. "Yes... Yes, it does."

"Could that be your name?" Lucy asked.

He stared at her, a frown between his brows, then gave an infinitesimal shake of his head. "I have no idea."

"It doesn't matter. David is perfect!" Bea pointed a triumphant finger at the page in front of her. "Beloved one." She looked at him with a beatific smile.

Things had gone far enough.

"Excuse us, I need to speak to my great-aunt for a moment." Taking Bea by the arm, Lucy led her out of the living room and cornered her in the hall, out of "David's" earshot.

"What are you doing?" she muttered under her breath. "That man's going to think you're nuts!"

"I don't care what he thinks about me." Bea looked up at her placidly. "But it's obvious he's perfect for you."

"Perfect for me! You *are* crazy," Lucy said in a furious whisper. "The man is a complete stranger. We know nothing about him."

"You just have to look into his eyes to see that he's sweet, generous and strong. There's integrity there."

Lucy gasped. "How can you possibly tell all that about him? He doesn't even know who he is, for heaven's sake!"

Bea wafted away her objections with a dismissive wave of her hand. "You young people today, you're so out of touch with your inner selves." She turned on her heel. "I'm going to go in and find out what David wants for breakfast."

Lucy put a hand on her great-aunt's arm. "Wait a minute. We have to call Dr. Marshall first and check. Maybe he should just have fluids."

"All I know is, there's a man in there who's weak as a kitten." Bea lifted her pointed chin with a no-nonsense air. "He needs to eat good wholesome food and I'm going to make sure he gets some."

She headed toward the living room with her assertive little strut, saying over her shoulder, "You call Dr. Marshall. I'm going to find out what I can entice him with."

With a sigh, Lucy picked up the heavy, old-fashioned black phone and spun the dial. It was just before eight, but the hall was still gloomy. Little light penetrated the stained-glass fanlight above the door, and the wind still howled and battered outside, sending showers of snow to rattle at the windows.

The old doctor answered the phone promptly, and after she'd described their patient's progress, he sounded unworried. The amnesia was probably temporary, he told her, and not uncommon after a head injury. Once the roads were cleared, he would be sending an ambulance.

"Just keep him quiet and make sure he gets plenty of rest," he added.

At that moment, Bea strutted by on her way to the kitchen, humming a little tune and practically skipping with delight.

Lucy watched her with a worried frown. It might be a good idea to have the doc check her out, too.

But she switched her attention to the phone as Dr. Marshall asked her if she'd called the police.

Lucy sighed, annoyed. "Why didn't I think of that?" From the moment she'd gotten involved with that ridiculous spell, her brain seemed to have gone on vacation.

Taking his advice, she called the station as soon as she said goodbye. Blaine was on duty.

"Lucy, I'm glad you called. How are you managing out there in this storm? Everything okay?" His warm, familiar voice was a welcome dose of calm reality.

"Fine, just fine. Well, actually, not so fine."

"What's wrong?"

As she explained what had happened, she could hear the clicking of computer keys at his end.

"No missing-person reports. No accidents reported, either," Blaine told her. "With the roads all closed down, I've got no way of taking this guy off your hands." He sounded concerned. "If you feel the least bit uneasy, call. I'll find some way to get out to you."

"Thanks, but I'm sure there'll be no need. He's quite harmless." That was a lie. She felt very vulnerable around him, the worst part being that he hadn't done anything. It was her.

At that moment, Bea trotted by with a tray. A mug of something steamed next to a covered plate. Folded beside it lay one of Bea's best linen napkins and a place setting of the monogrammed Weston silverware.

She shot Lucy a conspiratorial little grin and said softly, "Only the best for your beau."

With a groan, Lucy turned her attention to Blaine, who wanted a description.

When she'd finished giving him all the details about the man she could think of, there was a short pause at the other end of the line. She could sense Blaine hesitating. Then he cleared his throat.

"Listen, Lucy." The official tone vanished and his voice became softer. "If you don't already have a date for the Valentine's Dance, I'd really like it if you could come with me."

She felt a twinge of discomfort. "Oh, Blaine, I haven't changed my mind, you know."

"I'm not expecting you to. I've thought about what you said last time. I can't lie and say that I wasn't hoping for more. But if you just want to be friends, then that's all we'll be."

He sounded so sincere, she said warmly, "Then I'll be happy to go to the dance with you. Thank you for asking me."

But as she put down the phone, her mind churned with discontent. Was that really a good idea? She didn't understand herself these days.

It wasn't that she didn't like Blaine; he was very sweet. But as she had already told Bea, he didn't set the world on fire. Her thoughts immediately reverted to the man in her living room. Never mind the world, he set *her* on fire.

Just having him in her house was too disturbing. She rubbed her cold arms through her sweatshirt, and turned to go back into the living room. Time to focus on practical matters and will that unsettling feeling out of existence.

She found Bea perched on the edge of the couch, chatting with him as he lay propped higher against his pillows, finishing off a plate of scrambled eggs.

Lucy told them both what Dr. Marshall and the police had said.

The man put down his fork and looked up at her in dismay. "Don't worry, I'll find a way to get out of here today."

"You'll do nothing of the sort," Bea insisted indignantly. "Didn't you hear what the doctor said? You need plenty of rest and he'll send an ambulance for you when the weather clears."

He glanced at Lucy uncertainly, as if looking for her agreement with her great-aunt. "Well, that's very kind and hospitable of you, but I just couldn't continue to—"

"I'm afraid you have no choice," Lucy interrupted. He obviously felt like a nuisance, and she empathized with his plight. But what bothered her was how deeply she felt for him. She hardened herself against the feeling. "There's no way of getting out and there's no way of getting in. You have to stay here."

She had tried to avoid meeting his eyes, but there was something in his expression that kept her gaze riveted to his. Besides, she didn't know where else to look.

His chest was bare above the covers. Even the angry scar couldn't detract from the beauty of smooth golden skin and toned muscle that reminded her with uncomfortable acuity just how he had felt nestled against her—and that under those covers, he was entirely naked.

Oh, yes, she desperately wished he *could* leave here today. But where would he go? In spite of herself, she couldn't stop a twinge of worry as she noticed that his lean face looked pale and drawn. He'd been sitting up long enough.

"I think we should get you off the floor, and into a proper bed," she said briskly. "But I'm not sure you're strong enough to make it out of this room."

"I could try."

"No way! I don't want you to do anything that could cause complications." Despite Dr. Marshall's assurances, concussions were too serious to take lightly.

"Yes, and then I'll be on your hands even longer," he added quietly.

She felt her cheeks flush. It made her sound incredibly selfish, but it was the unpalatable truth. She cared about his health, but she cared more about the unsettling effect he had on her.

"Why don't we just put you on the couch?" she suggested finally.

He looked up at her, and even in the dim, curtained room, his eyes were very blue. "Whatever you say, but first I need to make a call."

"The phone's just out there in the hall," Bea piped up.

But Lucy knew he didn't mean that kind of call.

"There's...um...a bathroom off the kitchen," she said quickly, embarrassment bringing warmth to her cheeks. And he'd better be able to make it there. She couldn't possibly cope with the alternative. "Let me help you."

"No, no... I can manage." He flipped back the covers.

Lucy gasped and he swiftly pulled the quilts back in place. But even that brief sight of his lean, muscled body had been enough to send a stirring quiver of electricity through her.

A look of dismay crossed his face, and she said sharply, "I'll get your clothes."

Dashing out to the laundry room, she pulled his jeans from the dryer and hurried back with them.

Giving him the pants, she took Bea by the hand and yanked her. "We'll be back in a minute," she said over her shoulder.

"But he may need help," her great-aunt protested.

"I'll be fine," he said quickly.

"I'm sure he'll be fine," Lucy insisted. Why did this just keep on getting worse?

After a decent interval of a few minutes, they came back in to find he had the pants on, the fly zipped up, but the button left undone, as if he'd run out of steam.

He was hoisting himself unsteadily to his feet. Gripping the arm of the couch, he struggled upright, pain distorting his face for a moment. He clamped his lips into a grim line.

Obviously, he was the type of man who suffered in silence. That was a blessing, at least. Not that she didn't feel pity for him, but there was nothing worse than the sort who got sick and turned into a whining, bad-tempered child.

By the time he stood upright he was white around

the mouth from the effort. She hesitated, then went to help him—not a moment too soon.

As she put her arms around him, he swayed and leaned heavily on her, his head dropping against her shoulder. She staggered from his weight, but managed to hold him up.

With his bare chest pressed against her, his arms came up to encircle her, and he clung to her for support.

"I'm sorry, it's the dizziness...."

"It's all right. I understand." But it wasn't all right.

Her senses reeled. Now *she* was the one in danger of passing out. She could feel the hard contours of his body, the heat emanating from him. Her nipples tingled and burned, and heat unfurled between her thighs again. She held her breath, clenching every muscle, trying to quell the electric tremors racing through her.

Just when she thought she couldn't bear it for another second, he stiffened, moved away from her and stood straighter. He still kept one arm around her shoulder for support, obviously struggling to bear his own weight.

"Just give me a minute," he said grimly. "I'll be all right."

Whoever this man might be, he wasn't used to being helpless. With a stab of compassion, she suddenly realized how hard this must be for him, too, being so vulnerable among strangers. She felt an unwilling admiration. He certainly was tenacious, she had to give him that.

After a moment he let go completely, pushing her gently but firmly away. He took a step and swayed dangerously. She quickly reached for him and took his weight. Once again, involuntarily, her body tingled. But she steeled herself and tried to ignore the sensation.

Walking slowly, she helped him across the hall and into the kitchen. He didn't utter a sound, but she could tell by the way his lips were compressed, and how he squeezed his eyes shut, that his head injury must be intolerably painful. Still, despite his obvious weakness, he made his way with grim determination.

She only prayed he wouldn't need help when they reached their destination. Once they crossed the blue-tiled kitchen floor and reached the door to the bathroom beside the laundry area, he made it clear that he was equally anxious to manage the task independently.

"I'll take it from here," he said gruffly, leaning on the wall for support as he shut the door—but not before she saw another angry patch of scar tissue on his back. It was just above the shoulder blade, as if something had gone in one side of his body and out the other. Something like a bullet?

She felt an odd shiver of apprehension. But there could be any number of mundane explanations. She didn't feel particularly worried. After all, the man could barely walk, never mind pose a threat.

She hovered in the kitchen, aware of Bea bustling out of the living room and up the stairs, then pattering quickly down again a few minutes later. At length, the bathroom door opened and he came out, looking very pale as he supported himself for a moment by hanging on to the frame.

When he put his arm around her again, he seemed to

be leaning on her more heavily than before. The effort had obviously taken a lot out of him. A disturbing surge of anxiety coursed through her and she caught herself up abruptly; she didn't want to start worrying about him.

"I'm sorry, I must be very heavy for you to manage. You're so small." His voice was a little gruff, and his warm breath brushed her hair. She could sense the pain he was keeping to himself.

"Don't worry about me. I'm stronger than I look," she said gently, in spite of the strain.

When they finally got back into the living room, Bea had made up the long, broad couch into a comfortable-looking bed, piled with pillows and quilts.

Her great-aunt's face beamed with a pixieish smile as she held up a pair of maroon pajamas. "Look what I found in Georgie's old cedar chest!"

"Won't Georgie need them?" he asked uncertainly as they paused at the foot of the couch and Lucy helped him slowly lower himself down to a sitting position.

"Not anymore, I'm afraid. He's dead, you know." Bea sighed, and stroked the fine old silk. "It was quite a trip down memory lane, opening up that old box again. Remember the blond wig, Lucy?" She looked at her expectantly. "Oh, no, you probably don't, that would have been before your time." She let out a nostalgic sigh. "I did so love his Jean Harlow."

Lucy glanced at David. Despite his exhaustion, there was bemusement in his eyes, and she shuddered to think what he was making of all this.

"Georgie was my great-uncle," she quickly explained. "Bea's brother. He was...uh...in show business."

Bea tutted impatiently. "Now, Lucy, don't be so shy. David deserves to know all about the family accomplishments." She turned to him with pride. "Georgie was the best female impersonator on the vaudeville circuit. Do you know, he was so good, Errol Flynn asked him out on a date?"

David broke into a smile. "Wow! That good, huh?"

Although he was still drawn and pale, the smile sent a little tingle of appreciation through Lucy. His good-natured tolerance made him even more attractive. Perhaps her overblown response to him wasn't entirely her fault. Perhaps other women reacted to him like this, too.

Suddenly aware that she'd been lost in her thoughts, she turned quickly to her great-aunt. "I think it's time we let our patient get some *rest*, Bea," she said meaningfully. "Doctor's orders."

As quickly as possible, she hustled Bea out of the room. He would have to manage the pajamas on his own.

While Bea went into the kitchen, she headed upstairs for the safety of her studio.

All she could do was pray the storm would end soon. It *had* to. Then the ambulance would come and "David" would be someone else's responsibility. She just wanted this strange, unsettling man gone, and for life to get back to normal. Yesterday, she'd been a woman in charge of her own world. Or had that been an illusion, because nothing had ever challenged her strength before?

In just one night, she'd lost control of her impulses to a man who hadn't done a damn thing except sprawl unconscious on her doorstep. In just one night, she'd discovered part of herself she hadn't even known existed. What ever had possessed her? *Possessed!*

She shook off the ridiculous idea. There was no such thing as magic; only the power of suggestion. And it was obviously at work in her. It was that stupid phrase. *Send her the fulfillment of her woman's pleasure.*

The irony almost made her laugh out loud. The best orgasm she'd ever had, and the man was out cold. There was something sick about that, for sure. And worse, it hadn't been a one-time aberration. Every time she got close, she felt the same tingling, pulsing response that had been the harbinger of that cataclysmic event.

Everything had changed. Before, she'd been secure. Now she was running scared. But there was no escape. For the same reason he couldn't go anywhere, neither could she.

4

LUCY STARED AT THE rabbit she'd just drawn and gave a little gasp.

Her face burned and she quickly glanced behind her to make sure nobody was looking over her shoulder to see what she had done.

It was a perfectly natural little brown rabbit, complete with fluffy white tail—and a pair of piercingly blue, all-too-human eyes.

His eyes.

They were watching her the same way he watched her, with that quiet intensity that disturbed her so much...as if he could see right through her—which, thank God, he couldn't.

Quickly, she ripped the drawing into tiny pieces and tossed it into the wastebasket. Heaving a sigh, she leaned her elbow on the table and put her chin in her hand.

Why couldn't she get him out of her head?

All day, focusing on work had been impossible. She finally decided to channel her restlessness into a thorough cleaning of all the bedrooms.

After dinner, though, she knew that she absolutely had to get something done on this commission. Its end-of-February deadline loomed only five weeks away. But after four hours, all she had to show for her efforts was a wastebasket filled with crumpled paper.

Usually she had no problem buckling down to work. It was tearing herself away that was difficult. But that was something else that had changed, it seemed.

And the weather didn't help. The constant whistling of the wind around the eaves was getting on her nerves.

Jumping up from her chair, she walked over to the small window to stare out into the howling void. So much snow had built up around the frame that only a small, bare patch of glass remained.

It sounded as if the wind had died down a little, but not enough to get out skiing and work off some of her pent-up energy. Cabin fever—that was her problem. She was stuck indoors, with no escape from her incessant thoughts.

Maybe she should pour all this anxiety and unwelcome awareness into something constructive, she thought. The answer hit her like a revelation: She needed to paint.

She spun away from the window in a sudden fever of activity. Where were those canvases she'd picked up in town last week? She scanned the studio, the paintings stacked against one wall, and the long, cluttered bench at the end where she did her framing.

"Oh, no." She groaned, suddenly remembering. They were still on the back seat of her car. Oh, well, she wouldn't let that stop her. She had to do something, or she would drive herself crazy.

She headed softly down the narrow stairs. Glancing along the hall, she saw that Bea's bedroom light was out. It was past eleven; her great-aunt was undoubtedly asleep by now.

Treading lightly, she continued down the wide staircase. She was about to walk straight through into the kitchen, but instead, compelled by an impulse she couldn't ignore, she quietly crossed the shadowy hall to the living room.

Might as well check on their guest. He had slept all afternoon, and right through dinner, too. He hadn't even woken when she'd tiptoed in late that evening with a fresh jug of water and a bowl of grapes—just in case he stirred in the night and felt hungry.

Very slowly, so as not to make any noise, she opened one French door. She could barely make out a dark shape on the couch, but she could hear his quiet, even breathing.

That was good, wasn't it? Lots of sleep would make him heal faster. And then he could leave.

Turning, she hurried quietly down the hall and through the kitchen to the mudroom. Slipping on her boots and the heavy ski sweater she left on the hook by the closet, she went out the back door. She shut the screen door behind her, but left the inner door ajar to light her way.

The cold struck through her sweater and jeans while she hurried toward the garage as quickly as the drifts would allow. It was still snowing, although the wind had died down to only the occasional gust.

She went in by the side door, leaving it open. Aided by the feeble illumination of the house lights reflected on the snow, she groped for the switch on the wall, a few feet inside. As her cold fingers found it, a sudden gust of wind caught the door and slammed it shut with a resounding bang.

In pitch darkness, she flicked the switch. Nothing happened.

Damn, the bulb had burned out.

She sighed in annoyance as she made her way to the door again. Her hands were already stiff with cold as she found the knob, grasped it and turned. Nothing happened. The door refused to open.

She twisted it back and forth, and pushed hard, but the lock wasn't turning.

A needle of panic stabbed her, but she told herself to stay calm. Groping in the dark, she made her way to the big doors. She pushed, but they didn't move—just as she'd known they wouldn't.

This couldn't be happening. She couldn't be trapped in here.

Stumbling back to the side door, she tried the knob again, tried to push it open using all her weight and then began pounding on the door, yelling for Bea, even as the terrible realization hit her that doing so was futile.

Bea would never hear her, and neither would David. They were both asleep on the other side of the house. Her banging would never be heard through closed windows and over the howling of the wind.

Sheer mindless fear made her start to shake. *No!* She had to stop panicking right now and start to think. How could she get out of here? She had to; the cold was already unbearable. It must be minus thirty out here tonight, she thought, fighting down the fear once again.

Blinded by the dark, she moved back a foot or so, until she brushed against the old truck. Then, she threw herself hard against the door. Again and again, she slammed into it with all her weight, until her shoulder ached, but it didn't give an inch. The door was old, but it was solid.

Finally, she sagged against it in defeat, panting so hard that the freezing air seared her lungs.

Panic rose like a wave and threatened to engulf her. "No!" Her voice sounded unnaturally loud in the dead, cold silence.

She had to focus. Was the toolbox in the garage? With a sinking feeling, she remembered that it was still sitting in the laundry room, where she'd recently put up extra shelves.

But there had to be something she could use to force the door. Laboriously, she felt her way toward the workbench at the back of the cramped garage. In the utter blackness, she kept bumping into things: old furniture, camping equipment, the junk of years that had ended up piled against the garage walls.

She tripped and fell more than once, hurting her hands as she put them out to save herself. Would she even be able to pick up a tool? Her hands were frozen.

How long did it take to freeze to death?

Frantically, she turned her mind away from the thought as she bumped against the rusty fender of the old truck and clung to it for a moment. Reaching forward in the dark, she met the edge of the workbench.

Frantically, she felt her way over the rough surface for any kind of tool that could help her pry open the door, but nothing met her hands.

Suddenly she thought of the tire iron. She could jimmy open the door with it!

The sudden leap of hope withered as she remembered it was locked in the trunk of the car and the keys were in the house.

Her teeth were chattering now, her fingers numb. *No.* No, she couldn't die. Not within a hundred feet of her own home.

She groped her way back to the door and banged on it again, her hands like blocks of ice now, yelling herself hoarse. She began jogging on the spot, blowing on her hands, anything to try to keep the blood from freezing in her veins.

But the life was slowly draining out of her—she could feel it. And suddenly she wasn't cold any longer. Warmth and tiredness were stealing over her. At last, with a sob of relief, she sank onto the floor with her back against the door.

She wasn't going to die—not when she hadn't even begun to live.

David's face swam before her. So good to feel that sweet warmth stealing through her, to lean back and close her eyes, her thoughts slow and confused. How blissful not to feel anything anymore.

Suddenly the door burst open. David stood over her, silhouetted against the pale snow. "Oh, my God!" The freezing air clouded with his hoarse gasp. "Can you stand up?"

She opened her mouth to speak, but nothing came out. She tried to move, but every muscle refused to respond.

The next thing she knew, his arms were slipping around her. "Hold on, love. We'll get you warm soon." And then he was picking her up.

Somewhere in the dim recesses of her mind, she knew this was impossible. He couldn't do this. He was too hurt. Perhaps she was dreaming. A wonderful dream.

He carried her toward the house, and she could feel his arms trembling as they held her. When they entered the house, she was dimly aware that it was blissfully warm.

David got her to the kitchen and set her down on the braided rug by the stove. Lying in a heap on the floor, she could only watch with numb detachment as he reached up, turned on the oven and opened the door.

Then, turning to her, he crawled behind her and pulled her up between his legs, so that her back nestled against his chest. He wrapped his arms around her, holding her close, and rubbed his hands over her arms and thighs as she lay numbly, watching the oven elements begin to glow.

There was something enormously comforting about being enveloped by him like this. Gradually, she could feel the warmth of the oven seeping into her frozen body—and *his* warmth, the warmth of his body, and his hands that were rubbing life back into her limbs.

Feeling began to return—prickling pins and needles as the blood flowed back into her skin with burning discomfort. And along with that, the unbearable awareness of *him*—his scent, his touch, the feel of his body. Suddenly she began to shiver.

The touch of his hands now aroused an excruciating desire for him to touch her more completely. Another moment, and she would give herself away.

Abruptly, she sat up. He didn't try to stop her, but his soft voice came from behind her. "Are you all right now?"

She turned and moved away to kneel beside him on the braided rug. The enormity of what he had done finally came home to her—how much it must have cost him. She remembered the feeling of his arms trembling, the way he'd collapsed in front of the stove from the effort of carrying her.

"You saved my life. How can I thank you?"

"You don't have to. I was only repaying the favor." He was smiling, but his face looked pale and strained. "Tell me, is your life always this exciting? One dramatic rescue after another?"

He was making light of it, but she could see the pain in his eyes. It had been a herculean effort, and she felt utterly humbled.

"How did you know I was in trouble?" she asked.

"I heard you go out, but I didn't hear you come back in. Something told me to go find you. When I saw the back door open, I knew something was wrong. Then I saw your footsteps going out to the garage."

He made it sound like nothing. "I still can't believe you managed to carry me. You must have been in agony. How did you do it?"

"I had to," he said simply. "How do you feel now?"

"Probably a lot better than you do," she replied, with a rush of warmth and gratitude.

"You'll feel back to normal after a good night's sleep," he said quietly.

"You're the one who needs a good night's sleep. I'm sure it hasn't done you any good running around in the middle of the night rescuing foolish damsels in distress." Her voice cracked, spoiling her attempt to lighten the moment. He was clearly trying to downplay his own heroism, and was embarrassed by her thanks.

Rising shakily to her feet, she closed the oven door

and switched off the stove. Then she reached down and gave him her arm.

Steadying herself against him, she helped him get up. She gave him an anxious look. "I just hope this hasn't aggravated your head injury."

"I'll be fine." He let go of her and tried to stand on his own, but she could see him swaying.

"Please. Let me help you. It's the least I can do."

He gave her a long glance, then slung an arm around her shoulder. She hung on to his waist. As they began moving unsteadily down the hall, her legs shook.

David chuckled. "This is a little like the blind leading the blind, wouldn't you say?"

She couldn't help smiling. In spite of feeling acutely conscious of his nearness, a blissful sense of closeness and warmth washed over her.

They had reached the living room, and not a moment too soon. She tried not to think about how good the pressure of his body felt against hers.

As they reached the couch, she let him go with relief. Flicking on the small lamp on the end table, she watched him sink down on the makeshift bed.

"Now, is there anything I can get you before I go upstairs?"

In the soft lamplight, he smiled. "No. Nothing."

She hovered at the foot of the couch. "Then I'll let you get back to sleep."

"You're the one who needs to hit the sack. I've had about a week's worth of sleep today. I'm wide-awake now."

"Oh." Something inside her made her want to linger.

He lay back and pulled the covers over himself, then

gave her a questioning look. That comfortable feeling of camaraderie vanished. Once again she felt intensely aware of him. Her gaze darted nervously around the shadowy room, then she caught the gleam of his eyes watching her still, and blushed.

"Um...how do you feel? Other than wide-awake?" she asked awkwardly. Pretty inane, considering what he'd just been through.

"Believe it or not, my head doesn't hurt the way it did before. It's down to a steady pounding." He gave her a wry smile. "And I don't feel dizzy anymore."

"That's good," she said abstractedly.

The silence pressed in on her, and suddenly she realized how quiet it was indoors now. The incessant wind had died down for the first time in days. Was the storm over, or just taking a deep breath?

But in this room she felt it had only just begun. Her nerves wound tighter and tighter. There was no need to linger, and yet she felt reluctant to leave. Still, she should....

"In that case, I'll go back to bed. Good night."

"Good night," he said.

She turned away.

"Why were you out there, anyway?" His question made her turn back with ridiculous eagerness.

She felt absurdly hesitant. "I...I needed something from my car. The door slammed shut, and I couldn't open it. I thought I was going to die." A shudder went through her.

He said nothing for a moment, but there was something disquieting about the look in his eyes. Some kind of aura seemed to surround him, seemed to reach out

to touch her with an electric caress. It was almost...
supernatural.

"Is it just you and Bea here?"

Somehow she knew he was deliberately changing
the subject to get her mind off the morbid thoughts going through her head. "Yes."

"When did Georgie die?"

"About ten years ago."

"What about your parents?"

"They died when I was twelve," she said reluctantly.
This was one subject she hated to talk about, and
hardly ever did anymore.

He held her gaze, as if he were really interested in
the details of her life. More likely, he'd sensed her un-
reasonable reluctance to leave and felt obliged to make
conversation. She herself couldn't understand why she
needed to stay.

"Was that when you came to live with Bea and Georgie?"

She nodded.

A look of compassion came into his eyes. "How did
they die?"

Self-consciously, she crossed her arms and shifted
her weight. Pity always made her uncomfortable.
"Their plane went down in South America, in the
mountains of Patagonia. My grandmother was at the
controls. She and my grandfather died, too."

"I'm sorry."

"It was a long time ago," she said gruffly. "Fifteen
years."

"But it feels like yesterday, right? That sense of loss
never really goes away, does it?"

She stared at him. He actually understood. "How do you know this?"

He looked thoughtful, but said nothing for a moment. "I don't know how I know. I just know my parents aren't alive and I remember that sense of loss. I know what it feels like."

He suddenly looked up and the bleakness in his face clutched at her heart. How lonely he must feel.

"I'm sure you must," she said gently. "After all, you've lost your whole world."

Suddenly his hard mouth curved in a cheerful grin, and mocking amusement made his eyes even more intensely blue. "Now, don't you go feeling sorry for me. I consider myself very lucky. I couldn't have ended up with two nicer people than you and Bea."

There was something very warm in his expression that made her heart skip a beat. She should go upstairs right now and stop willfully heading down this very dangerous path. But instead, she just stood there, gazing down at him.

He put one hand under his head to raise himself a little against the pillows. "How long has she been trying to find you a husband?"

The abrupt question took her by surprise, but suddenly she realized she wasn't embarrassed anymore.

Her mouth lifted in a smile. "She thinks I've been a spinster too long, and before I get too old and dried up—"

He began to chuckle. "I'm sorry." His husky voice in the dimly-lit room made her skin prickle. "I can't imagine anyone less dried up."

A flood of warmth began in her toes and spread through her like wildfire. She sharply reminded herself not to be stupid. He was just being polite. What was the man supposed to do, agree?

"Anyway, she thinks I'm running out of time. I'd better get myself a man. And if I won't, she will."

"But she's never been married, right?"

"That's exactly why she thinks it's so important for me. When she was about twenty, she got engaged to an idealistic young guy who volunteered for the Spanish Civil War. He got himself killed, and Bea was heartbroken. She hid herself away, content to stay here with Georgie. She realized too late how much she'd missed. She doesn't want to see me follow in her footsteps."

"So why aren't you married?" he asked, then abruptly closed his eyes and pressed his fingers against the lids. When he opened them again, he looked contrite. "I'm sorry, I don't know what possessed me to ask such a personal question."

"That's all right, I'm used to it." But suddenly she felt absurdly defensive. "Around here, everyone thinks it's a woman's sole destiny. Do you think that, too?"

"Not at all, but I just can't believe that someone like you—" He stopped self-consciously. "Never mind, it's none of my business."

She felt a ridiculous glow of pleasure at his unspoken compliment. All at once it was very important that he understand. "I haven't met anyone I wanted to marry. And I enjoy my independence too much to give it up for someone I'm not madly in love with."

Trying to act casual, she leaned one hip back against the high arm of the couch. Why was she telling him any of this? Why was it so important that he understand?

He gave her a quietly penetrating look. "But why do

you feel you'd have to give up your independence at all?"

For a moment she was taken aback and unsure how to answer. With a shock, she realized that she'd never questioned her own belief. Then she rallied. "That seems to be the way it works."

"I guess so, in some cases. But I can't imagine that happening to you." Warmth and admiration shone in his eyes, making her knees weaken. "You're a strong person, Lucy Weston."

If that were true, why was she glad to be leaning against the couch so she didn't fall down? She had a horrified realization: This attraction went beyond sex.

Somehow she managed a shaky laugh. "Maybe I'm too strong. Men seem to prefer women who are a little more...pliable."

"Some men. But I can't think of anyone who wouldn't want someone who was kind, caring and affectionate, not to mention pretty."

He smiled. She liked the way his eyes crinkled at the corners. He looked like a man who smiled a lot. Or were those narrowed eyes more accustomed to scanning distant hills or the sweep of the ocean?

What was she doing? Was she crazy? The last thing she needed was to start wondering about him, theorizing about what sort of man he was...or, God forbid, to romanticize him.

She didn't *want* to know anything about him. She didn't want to stand here in the middle of the night, telling him all about herself. But in the soft light, his gaze seemed to reach right down into her soul—as if she didn't need to tell him anything; he could read it for himself.

Suddenly it was difficult to breathe. A rush of heat flamed up into her face. He was just being gallant, and she was stupid enough to take it seriously. With any luck, he would soon be on his way and she would never see him again. But he wouldn't be leaving today. He wouldn't be leaving soon enough.

A shiver of foreboding raced over her, making all the little hairs on her arms stand on end.

"I think I'd better go to bed now." This time, she had better do it.

"There's just one thing I wish you'd tell me before you go."

She paused, suddenly wary. "What's that?"

"Your great-aunt behaves as if I were expected. Is there something I don't know about? Something about me?"

"No... No, nothing like that," she said hastily. God only knew what was going through his mind. What the heck, she might as well tell him. He had a right to know something about the insane setup he'd landed in.

"I told you that Bea thinks I need a husband. For the past six months she's been doing her best to find me one." She sighed, feeling her color rise. "I've had to endure endless teas, and a couple of disastrous blind dates. Bea was getting desperate. Desperate enough to...to cast a spell." She said the last words hurriedly, hoping he wouldn't take them in.

"A spell!" His eyebrows rose a fraction, and she could see his lips twitch with amusement. "As in magic?"

She nodded her head, and admitted heavily, "And I helped her do it."

His brows rose even higher, and his eyes twinkled with laughter. "You helped?"

"I was only humoring her," she defended quickly, knowing her admission made her look pathetically desperate. "The trouble is, she thinks the spell worked because you landed on our doorstep a few minutes later."

"Ah... Now everything's beginning to make sense."

"I'm glad it makes sense to you," she muttered. Thank God he didn't know it all. "I hope you realize Bea isn't about to let up. I'm sorry, but it's liable to get worse."

"Don't worry about it." There was a warm vibrancy in his husky voice, like sandpaper on velvet in the dimly-lit room. "Putting up with Bea's idiosyncrasies is the least I can do. You saved my life."

"And you saved mine. So we're even."

"In China, they say if you save a person's life, you're responsible for them for as long as they live."

His quiet voice sent a shiver of apprehension running through her. "Well, fortunately, we don't live in China. We're responsible for ourselves."

Tomorrow, the storm would have passed and he would be gone. And then that horrible tingling current that ran up her spine every time she got close to him would go away.

And yet, it had felt oddly comfortable to talk to him so openly. Didn't they say it was easier to tell things to a stranger?

And this dark stranger was completely outside her experience, even outside reality. Was that what drew her to him—that kept awareness simmering inside her when he was near?

Once again she felt a tremor of apprehension. She must stay as far away from him as possible. Starting now. And this time she really, *really* meant it.

"I think it's time I got to bed," she said quietly. "Good night."

She began to turn away again, but he sat up, reached out and took her hand. At the touch of his fingers on hers, her heart seemed to stop beating for a second, then launched into a rapid, erratic pace.

Before she knew what he was doing, he kissed her hand. It was only a light, gallant gesture of appreciation, she knew that. But the brief pressure of his warm lips sent a river of fire flooding through her veins.

If he pulled her down to him, she would be lost. Terrified by the intensity of the feeling, she yanked her hand away, turned and ran from the room, fleeing up the stairs.

LONG AFTER HE'D HEARD Lucy's footsteps patter up the stairs and cross the floor above his head, he lay awake, listening to the sounds of the old house in the darkness. The wind had sunk to a faint, comforting rustle, and once again the furnace rumbled into life somewhere down below.

Was she still awake up there?

Her hand had felt so right in his, her skin so soft against his fingers, so satiny against his lips.

A long, confused sigh escaped him. Whatever urge had made him kiss her hand had become an overpowering impulse to pull her into his arms and taste that soft pink mouth. He groaned.

Holding her, rubbing life back into her body, had been a kind of torture. He had ached for her with an acute desire that was all wrong. But at least fighting that need had given him something to focus on other than the terrible pain in his head.

What was happening to him?

His emotions seemed to be running wild; they were as overblown and fantastic as everything else in the past twenty-four hours.

He mustn't trust these feelings. They were all part of this long, crazy dream. A dream that had begun by waking up beside the most beautiful woman he'd ever seen. She had to be the most beautiful woman he'd ever seen, but he couldn't be sure of that. He couldn't be sure of anything.

Then there was Bea, wafting in and out like some kind of hallucination. And he, himself: sleeping, waking, sleeping, stumbling through the snow, rescuing Lucy from certain death. It all seemed like a dream— especially the desire that took him over when she was near.

And it wasn't just desire. She touched him. It was obvious that she'd been too frightened to go back to her room right away. He'd wanted to take her in his arms and comfort her, but he'd settled for just talking until her fears dissolved. And besides, he'd wanted her to stay.

He groaned and pressed a hand to his eyes. Had he ever felt like this about a woman before? He must have. Was there a woman in his life? He searched his mind for something—some image, some flash of memory to guide him. It was no good.

But he knew one thing: He had no business feeling these impulses, much less acting on them.

Perhaps these overblown emotions were just his

mind's way of compensating for the black hole of his memory. And yet now and then, there were flashes... And that dream he'd woken from just before he heard Lucy going out.

He'd been walking along a forest path with a group of children. All was drowsy peacefulness; the sun shone down through the trees. But suddenly, somewhere on the edge, just out of sight, an unseen terror lurked. A feeling of helplessness had swept over him. He couldn't protect all the children from the approaching horror.

Cold fear had gripped him, and then he'd known he was awake, struggling desperately against the weight holding his lids shut. He must open his eyes. The terror had followed him out of the dream; it was there in the room with him.

And suddenly his eyes were open. He could make out the shapes of the old-fashioned furniture in the dimly-lit room. Nothing else was there. Fighting to slow his racing heart, he'd heard the sound of Lucy's footsteps in the hall, and the back door opening.

Thank God he'd woken when he did.

He stared up into the shadows. Lucy might not believe that saving someone's life made you responsible for them, but he did. Now he was obliged to keep Lucy safe—from himself.

5

LUCY ROLLED OUT OF BED, feeling like ten miles of bad road.

It was only 7:00 a.m. Normally she wouldn't see this time of day unless she stayed up to meet it. But all night long she'd been chasing sleep, and she couldn't even blame it on the storm.

The wind had ebbed around three. Then it had been too quiet, with nothing to distract her from the tormenting, conflicting thoughts and feelings going through her head.

Last night David had not only saved her life, he'd done it by risking his own. And something about him had made her open up and tell him things she'd never told anyone before. No wonder she'd tossed and turned.

There was something disturbing about how comfortable she had felt with him.

Then he'd kissed her hand.

Ambling over to the window, she pulled open the drapes and saw with relief that the snow had stopped.

Outside, the branches of the blue spruce sagged under the weight of a thick white blanket, and as far as her eye could see, the whole world lay muffled under the same smooth porcelain quilt. The fields and fences, the Johnsons' farmhouse and barn, were all nearly obliterated.

The only contrast to this rolling blue-white panorama was offered by the line of bare maples bordering the road. That and the gray eastern sky, shot with delicate ribbons of pink and rose, heralding the almost-forgotten sun.

Her breath clouded the cold glass as she heaved an anxious sigh. It scared her, the way her emotions seemed beyond her control when she was around him. She'd never felt this way with anyone before. The last time she could remember feeling this vulnerable had been that terrible year when her parents had died.

But it wasn't David's fault she felt this way. He wasn't doing anything. And here she'd been treating him like a leper, at a time when he most needed care and compassion. After what he'd done for her, surely the least she could do was keep her own wayward emotions under control and show him some kindness—make him feel comfortable in a strange house.

She stumbled down the hall to the bathroom. After a hot shower, she pulled on a cozy sweater and leggings.

It was her own stupid imagination, making her think she could still feel the imprint of his firm lips on her hand, no matter how much she soaped and scrubbed.

Heading down the stairs, she swung around the newel post and stopped short with a gasp, startled to see him standing in the living-room doorway, hanging on to the doorjamb.

"Good morning," he said quietly.

Suddenly shy and self-conscious, she dropped her gaze, unsure where to look.

His pajama top hung open, revealing the smooth, muscular curves of his chest. He was unshaven and disheveled, and still looked disturbingly attractive, even in those absurd silk pajamas. The legs were too short, and they hung too loosely on his lean hips. But to her chagrin, they didn't diminish his air of tough, quiet masculinity one bit.

"You don't even want to look at me this morning, and I don't blame you," he said ruefully.

"What?" She glanced up, startled.

He looked apologetic. "I know I made you feel uncomfortable last night when I kissed your hand. I did it without thinking—just trying to show my gratitude—but I guess I should have done it another way. I don't want to make you feel uncomfortable."

What would he think if he knew she'd rushed out of the room last night so she wouldn't make a fool of herself by asking for more? What would he say if he knew that the reason she avoided looking at him now was because doing so only made her want him?

"I don't feel uncomfortable," she lied valiantly. Then she looked at him more closely and realized that it wasn't a lie. Suddenly, concern overwhelmed her.

Beneath the shadow of his beard, his face was pale and drawn. It didn't take a doctor to recognize that his exertions last night had taken their toll.

She eyed him, her worry growing. "You look dreadful this morning, and I know it's all my fault."

"No, it's not." He gave her a grin, in spite of the pain in his eyes. "I think I'm just one of those people who look like hell every morning."

Yeah, right. And she was the archbishop of Canterbury.

Resolutely, she crossed the hall to him and slipped an arm around his waist. "Lean on me."

The warm, musky scent of him swamped her. She

had to steel herself to keep from drowning in the heady sensation.

For a second, he stiffened with resistance. Then he sighed, put his arm around her shoulder, and sagged against her. It seemed like the most natural thing in the world to put her other arm around him and hold him steady.

But once again, a quiver of acute longing raced through her. Through the silk of the pajama top, she could feel the heat of his flesh, the smooth contours of hard muscle. She bit down on her bottom lip, and the pain brought tears to her eyes, but it didn't erase the unnatural surge of desire.

"You're a marvelous woman, Lucy. An angel of mercy. Are you a nurse or something like that?"

Stunning warmth flowed to every inch of her, taking her breath away. "No, far from it. I illustrate books."

Keeping this feeling in perspective wasn't as easy in practice as it was in theory.

"Well, you make a very good nurse. You're very comforting." His muffled voice was slow and drowsy, and she realized that he was talking to distract himself from the pain, from the effort it cost to move along the hallway, even at this snail's pace.

"What kind of books?" he asked.

"Huh?"

"What kind of books do you illustrate?"

"Mostly children's books," she answered distractedly, much too aware of the soft brush of his chin against her hair, the pleasurable weight of his arm across her shoulder.

"You'll have to show me."

"When you're better." They were nearing the

kitchen, and she could hear Bea humming tunelessly, thankfully bringing her back to mundane reality. "Listen, please do me a favor and don't say anything to my great-aunt about last night. I don't want to worry her."

"Gotcha."

The intimacy of his tone made her look up at him. His warm smile held conspiratorial amusement that shook her badly.

The worst thing about this out-of-control sensation was that it made her feel good—as if she just wanted to let go and see where it would take her. But she couldn't afford to do that.

At the door of the kitchen, he paused and straightened away from her. "I can manage from here, thanks."

"Good morning!" Bea turned from the stove to give them both a wide, expectant smile. "Did everyone sleep well?"

"Like a log," Lucy lied cheerfully.

"And you, David? That couch must be uncomfortable. Now that you're on your feet, we must see about getting you upstairs to a real bed." Bea's bright, shrewd gaze swept over him as he slowly crossed the kitchen, heading toward the bathroom.

Lucy jumped in quickly. "The storm is over and the roads will soon be cleared. I'm sure David's anxious to find out where he's from and go home. He may not even be here tonight."

That should have been a cheering thought, but suddenly the prospect of life getting back to normal didn't seem so appealing.

"We'll see," Bea said cryptically. The oven timer went off, sending her scurrying for the pot holders.

Automatically, Lucy took the old Blue Willow platter from the hutch and set it on the table. The rich aroma of Morning Glory muffins filled the kitchen as Bea took the tray from the oven and began popping the hot muffins onto the platter.

"Now, I've already eaten, so it's just you and David. Make sure he eats something." She set the empty tray on the counter and began unfastening her white apron.

"Where are you going?" Lucy asked in alarm as Bea hung her apron on the hook beside the stove.

"Upstairs. I've fallen behind in my Esperanto lessons. I must get caught up."

"Do you have to do that now?" Panic gripped her. It would be much easier to treat David like a human being if there was another human being around.

A sound from behind made her turn to find him standing in the open doorway watching her. Her cheeks tingled. How much had he heard? She knew very well what it must have sounded like. This was the sort of thing that made him feel unwelcome, which she'd vowed not to do anymore.

Bea saw him too, and shot him a brilliant smile. "There you are, dear. Lucy was just about to carry your breakfast into the living room for you."

"If it's all the same to you, I'd rather join you at the table. It may help me feel human again." He gave Bea a self-deprecating smile and Lucy felt her heart miss a beat.

She snapped out of her distraction. "My great-aunt's absolutely right. You should be back in bed. I'll come and keep you company."

She pasted on a reassuring smile, proud of herself for overcoming her instinctive desire to run away.

Why did he have to be so attractive? And what was it about him, anyway? His features were regular, but hardly striking, except for those intensely blue eyes. He wasn't the type who would stand out in a crowd, but something about him reached her in the most primitive, frightening way.

But she was going to keep her resolution and not treat him like a leper. Besides, keeping him in bed was less of a distraction than having him up and about.

With a jab of remorse, she went to help him again. Putting her arm around him, she steeled herself against the feeling of contact. He'd buttoned the pajama top, but that didn't help one bit.

She smiled up at him. "Come on, I'll help you back to bed."

As he put his arm across her shoulders, she gritted her teeth. His touch felt much too good for comfort.

After getting him to the darkened living room, she quickly fluffed up the pillows and fixed the makeshift bed. He sank down onto it gratefully.

He didn't need a whole stack of bedding anymore. She pulled up the warmest quilt and tucked it in around him. She looked up and caught his gaze, which was filled with warm amusement, and she realized how maternal her gesture had been. She felt keenly embarrassed, and disturbed at the way he roused her protective instincts.

"I'll go get us some breakfast." She backed away, glad to put a little distance between them, even temporarily. If she was going to win this fight with herself, she had to know when to retreat.

HE BREATHED A SIGH of relief as she left the room, glad to have a moment to collect himself. When she'd tucked the quilt in around him, the solicitous gesture had touched him much too deeply. It had just been her automatic response to his condition, he told himself—nothing personal. He couldn't let himself want that kind of caring from her.

But could he forget the feel of her body lying next to him, soft but strong; or the scent of her, an intoxicating blend of soap and baby powder? It was an attraction too strong to fight in his feeble state.

In a world where nothing was normal, he didn't know whether this reaction to her felt good or not. He just knew it was uncomfortably intense. He had to keep his emotional distance and, most important, a little perspective.

By the time she returned a few minutes later, with a laden tray, he felt a little more under control. But he couldn't stop watching her.

"I hope you don't mind fruit and muffins for breakfast," she said brightly, but he could still sense her tension.

She set her load on the coffee table and pushed the table right up beside the couch, every movement graceful and feminine.

"Sounds great." He wasn't particularly hungry, but he had to eat to build up his strength. That way he could get out of here as quickly as possible, and relieve her of the nuisance of having a sick stranger in the house.

"You're easy to please," she said with a smile and sank to her knees on the other side of the table.

Everything about her pleased him. But danger lay in

those kinds of thoughts. And suddenly, he was very glad they had the coffee table between them.

Tearing his gaze away from her, he took a plate and helped himself to a muffin. "So tell me about this beautiful house of yours," he said, relieved to have found a safe topic of conversation. "Has it been in the family a long time?"

It seemed he wasn't the only one relieved to have something innocuous to talk about. He sensed her relax a little as she began to talk about the house while she ate.

It was built in the 1890s, she said, on the site of a log cabin. Frederick Weston had been the first pioneer to clear the bush, and the village of Hazeldene had been named after his wife, Bea's great-great-grandmother.

"When Bea was a child, this was a working farm," Lucy explained, her beautiful face animated as she recounted the family history. "But now she rents out the land and runs the house as a bed-and-breakfast, catering mostly to tourists on their way up north to Georgian Bay, or to the skiing at Blue Mountain. It's not for the money so much as the opportunity it gives her to meet people. We get mostly families, and Bea loves kids."

In the soft lamplight, he saw the shadow of a smile curve her beautifully molded lips. There was something so exotic about her, with her dark hair and glowing green eyes, that sent an electric current buzzing through his veins. He had to fight the urge to reach out and caress her soft, peach-tinted skin.

Get control of yourself, stupid!

"No wonder Bea's so keen for you to get married. I bet she'd like some great-grandnieces and -nephews."

The thought of her being married gave him an unpleasant jolt, but he pushed it aside. He had to remember he had no part in Lucy's life, and never would.

"You've got that right." With a wry, embarrassed
smile, she looked down at the empty paper muffin cup
in her hand and folded it over and over onto itself.
"And as you know, she'll go to any lengths to make it
happen."

"You're not kidding," he said lightly, trying to ignore a surge of inexplicable resentment. "Most people
would try a dating service, or the personal ads."

"Personal ads!" She clapped a hand to her forehead
with a shudder of dismay. "Oh, Lord, don't remind
me."

"Don't tell me." He shook his head in mock horror.

She nodded. "I'm afraid so. Just before Christmas,
Bea put an ad in one of the Toronto weeklies without
telling me."

"So what happened?" He tried to make the question
sound casual.

Lucy didn't quite meet his eyes, but she was smiling.
"The first letter she got— Well, there was a Polaroid
with it that went straight into the fire before I even had
a chance to see it. She pulled the ad the very next day.
Now, as far as Bea's concerned, the personals are only
for sexual deviants and the totally desperate."

He laughed, with a crazy surge of relief. Then suddenly he didn't feel like laughing anymore. "I'm glad
Bea has given up on that, at least. It's too risky." But it
wasn't just the risk; it was the thought of her with another man that bothered him.

"Yeah, she came to that conclusion herself. So is it
any wonder she thinks you're a gift from God?" Under

the flippancy, he could hear her underlying self-consciousness. He got her message loud and clear; she didn't want him thinking that she shared Bea's opinion.

Despite the fact that she was much less aloof today, it didn't mean her feelings toward him had changed. More likely, she had warmed toward him out of gratitude for last night.

Last night. He shuddered to think what could have happened if he hadn't woken up. He could have lost her.

He caught himself with a jolt. *Lost her?* He'd never *had* her. But he wanted her, and that was a dangerous way to feel. There was no way he could acknowledge this attraction, never mind do anything about it.

WHEN THEY HAD FINISHED eating, Lucy picked up the tray and got to her feet to leave, torn between relief and reluctance.

David put the covers aside and went to get up off the couch with an animal grace that brought that simmering awareness to the boil again.

"What are you doing?" she asked quickly.

His blue eyes met hers, warm and open. "The least I can do is help you clean up breakfast."

"You stay here." Once again, she felt the need to put some distance between them. "Cleaning up the kitchen is my job," she told him with a determined smile. "Bea won't let me cook. She says it's a crime what I do to food."

"Now, Lucy, you're exaggerating just a little!" With a patter of slippers on the wood floor, Bea came bustling into the room. "It's not a crime, more like a misdemeanor."

She marched over to the couch and leaned over David solicitously. "How do you feel, now that you've had something to eat?"

With a gentle touch, she brushed the hair off his forehead and straightened the collar of his pajamas, exactly as if he were a small boy to be fussed over.

In spite of herself, an unwilling smile curved Lucy's mouth. They made an amusing picture—the tiny bird-like figure of Bea, and this tall, lean and disturbingly masculine stranger. She couldn't help noticing that he docilely accepted Bea's attentions, without any of the mocking amusement her own efforts had drawn.

But then again, Bea's motives *were* purely maternal. The same couldn't be said for hers. Perhaps he'd sensed her rapacious lust.

Even now, her gaze dwelt on his broad shoulders and the way the silk clung to the curves of his chest. She turned guiltily away, clutching the tray more tightly as she hurried out to the kitchen.

There had to be some explanation for this strange, compelling feeling that had her in its grip. And it certainly wasn't magic. But it had all begun the night that man landed on their doorstep.

What was it, then? Sexual deprivation? After all, it had been six months since Ethan left. But when had sex ever been that important to her before? Only since that fateful, ill-judged moment when she'd lain down next to David and discovered the depths to which she could sink.

The phone rang and she rushed into the hall to answer it, glad to have something else to think about. It was Dr. Marshall, calling to say that as soon as the road was clear, the ambulance would be on its way. She felt duty-bound to offer to drive David in herself, but the doctor insisted that with a head injury, transport by ambulance would be much safer.

She put down the phone with an overwhelming feeling of...ambivalence.

She should be relieved. He would be gone, and at last, life could go back to normal. But instead, she felt anxious and dissatisfied. What was the matter with her? Didn't she want to see him go?

Of course, she did. Right from the start she'd known he was a danger to her. But at the door to the living room, she paused.

The quilts lay neatly folded at one end of the couch and David lay at the other, propped upright against the pillows. He was holding a skein of purple yarn between his hands while Bea perched in the overstuffed armchair on the other side of the coffee table, rapidly winding it into a ball. They weren't even talking; just sitting in companionable silence.

A spurt of alarm made her bite her lip. He was clearly very comfortable with her great-aunt. And just as clearly, Bea had already become attached to him.

What would happen when he vanished as suddenly as he had appeared?

Once again she sighed. All he had done was upset their lives. The sooner he left, the better.

6

"GOOD NEWS," SHE SAID, with forced brightness as she walked into the living room.

"What's that, my dear?" Her great-aunt looked up at her with a loving smile, while David just watched her with that quiet intensity she was beginning to know so well.

Once again that breathless awareness filled her, and she felt uncomfortably vulnerable. She *was* glad he was finally leaving.

"Doc Marshall says the ambulance should arrive sometime this afternoon, depending on how quickly they get the plows out." It took real effort to sound cheerful.

"Good," Bea replied, nodding placidly. "The sooner we have you checked out, the sooner we can relax and be less anxious."

It was obvious Bea was assuming he would be coming back, and Lucy didn't feel like pointing out that he would probably be hospitalized for a few days, and then go on his way.

She caught him still watching her with an enigmatic, quietly probing look. What had her unguarded expression given away?

"I'd better clear the laneway, or the ambulance will never get to us," she said quickly as she turned to leave the room.

"What can I do to help?" The sound of his husky voice sent a tremor through her.

Without looking at him, she frantically shook her head. "Nothing. I can manage. I do it all the time."

On shaky legs, she hurried out to the mudroom and pulled her down-filled black parka from the peg. As she slipped her arms into the sleeves, his voice, close behind her, startled her.

"At least give me a shovel so I can clear the walk and the steps for you."

"I don't think so," she said shortly, without turning. She didn't want to look at him for fear he would see her ambivalence about him leaving. "I'm sure Dr. Marshall would say you shouldn't exert yourself like that."

"I'm sure Dr. Marshall would also appreciate that I feel dangerously emasculated, and that can't be good for my spirits."

His dry tone made her turn her head to glance at him. He was smiling, with a warm intensity in his eyes that captured hers and made her smile back. Once again, she could appreciate how he must hate feeling so helpless. She knew that feeling herself, and despised it.

"I'm sorry," she said more gently. "This must be really difficult for you."

His smile became a little teasing. "That's better. I was afraid I'd have to leave here without getting you to look at me again."

"I guess I've just been a little distracted. I'm worried about Bea—how she's going to take it when you leave." That was only half the reason, and she couldn't bring herself to look at him for too long, in case he guessed the other half.

Glancing down, she fumbled with the zipper of her jacket. His closeness made her fingers clumsy.

"I'm sure she'll be fine. She's a tough old bird. And I hope you're not worrying that because of all this magic stuff she's losing it. Nothing could be further from the truth." Then suddenly there was something wistful in his voice that made her glance up again. "But I guess you'll be glad to see me go."

"I'll be glad to see you in competent hands," she answered carefully, and bent over to pull on her boots.

When she straightened, he was still looking at her, his expression enigmatic. What was he thinking? she wondered, then abruptly turned her thoughts off.

She didn't want to know what he was thinking. It didn't matter what he was thinking. He was going to be gone soon. If only she didn't feel so bleak.

"Well, I'd better get out there," she mumbled awkwardly, not quite meeting his gaze, and hurried out.

Closing the door behind her, she stopped for a moment. The cold pinched her cheeks and ears. She'd run out before putting on her red knitted hat and gloves, still clutched in her hands.

But right now she didn't care about anything except gasping in a few lungfuls of the crisp, invigorating air in an effort to steady her nerves and clear her head. Being close to him made her feel... *Claustrophobic.* That was the word! He made her confused, so that she didn't know what she felt anymore.

She plodded through the knee-deep snow, noticing that already there were signs of life returning: the delicate hieroglyphics of bird prints on the snow; even a rabbit track disappearing under the bare lilacs at the side of the house. They were welcome reminders that life was getting back to normal after the storm.

Quickly, she cleared the drift in front of the big double doors and got into the crowded garage that held the truck and the Honda. She felt a sick jolt to see the side door standing open. This could have been her tomb. The thought made her shudder with superstition.

It took only twenty minutes to clear the long, tree-lined drive with the plow mounted on the front of their ancient pickup. The road to town had already been cleared, so now there was nothing to stop the ambulance from reaching them.

Just as she finished clearing the front steps, she heard the sound of a vehicle on the highway. Shading her eyes, she looked down the road to see the ambulance approaching.

Relief poured through her. It was over. The emotional roller-coaster ride she'd been on ever since this man had turned up was almost at an end. Maybe now she could recover her equilibrium.

She hurried inside to discover that David had dressed in his own clothes and stood at the living-room window looking out. He gave her a rueful smile as she came in.

"Looks like this is it." There was something disquieting in his eyes.

With a stab of guilt, she realized that she'd been dwelling on her own petty concerns. What about David? After all, his future was a blank. Where would he go from here?

On the other hand, maybe she *should* go back to her own petty concerns. Worrying about him was too disquieting. Whatever happened, he would be fine. He was a strong, independent man; he could take care of himself.

He was staring out the window again. She followed his gaze. Outside, a clump of snow fell softly from the roof of the porch and landed on the wooden railing. Suddenly he turned, with a stricken, faraway look on his face.

"What's wrong?" she asked quickly.

He focused on her with a frown. "I suddenly had this flash," he said slowly, "of being snowed in, in a cabin in the mountains."

"What do you remember about it?"

His expression became faraway again. "There was a pine forest all around, and you could see right across the valley to this massive peak that kept getting lost in the clouds."

He painted such an appealing, vivid picture, she found herself wishing she could go somewhere like that. Strange, considering she'd never felt any particular urge to travel before. In fact, the thought of leaving this house, and Bea, had always filled her with a faint sense of anxiety.

"Yes, I remember that cabin. It had a big old fieldstone fireplace that kept us warm. I think we were stranded there—there was a bunch of us."

"Do you remember where it was? Who you were with?" She felt a stab of unreasoning jealousy. Was one of those people somebody special in his life?

Frustration filled his eyes, and he shook his head in defeat. "I have no idea. But I do remember how remote and unspoiled that spot was."

Remote and unspoiled and very romantic, no doubt.

The sound of the knocker brought her to her senses. She had no right to feel jealous.

She rushed quickly into the hall and threw open the door to see two ambulance attendants standing on the porch with a stretcher.

"Miss Weston?"

"Right this way." She opened the door wider as they wheeled the gurney past her into the front hall.

"You won't be needing that." David eyed the stretcher with a scowl. "I'm quite capable of walking out of here."

"But you'll need these." Bea came tripping down the stairs with her wallet in one hand, a pair of sunglasses in the other, and a coat over one arm.

She handed him the glasses. He took them from her with a smile and slipped them on. "Thanks."

Then she held out the coat. "Georgie was a small man. I know this won't fit very well, but it's better than nothing."

He put on the navy cashmere topcoat. As Bea had predicted, the arms were far too short and the hem didn't even reach his knees, but that didn't seem to bother him at all.

He leaned down and gave Bea a peck on the cheek. "I'll make sure you get this back. Thank you for everything you've done for me." He included Lucy in his warm smile, then turned and walked out, with the ambulance attendants following.

Lucy was about to close the door when Bea joined the procession, with her coat on.

"Where are you going?" Lucy stared at her with a sinking feeling. As if she didn't already know.

"You don't expect us to abandon our dear David at a

time like this," Bea said matter-of-factly. "Of course we'll follow in the car."

Lucy gave a resigned sigh. She'd had no intention of going with him and prolonging the moment of final leave-taking. There was no reason to feel this senti-mental about a man she'd known for just over a day.

But it didn't matter what she wanted. If she refused, Bea would be quite prepared to drive herself into town. And the little matter of not having a license had never stopped her before. Without a word, Lucy went out to the garage to warm up the sturdy old Honda.

They followed the ambulance along the snowy road for the two-mile drive into town through the wintry countryside. The sky had cleared and big puffy clouds were racing across the blue canvas. The sun glared off snow-laden trees, making purple shadows under the frosted evergreens. Mountains of snow lined the roads, and as they reached town there seemed to be rosy-faced kids in every front yard, sliding down the snow-banks, hauling sleds or building snowmen.

If only she could enjoy the beauty of it all, and stop worrying about...that man in the ambulance ahead.

When they reached the small district hospital on the other side of town, Dr. Marshall was already waiting for them.

"So this is our mysterious patient." His voice boomed across the entryway.

Tall, gray-haired and good-humored as ever, the doctor introduced himself and led David through the big double doors leading to Emergency.

Bea hurried along beside him, but the doctor gave her a challenging look. "And just where do you think you're going? You'll stay right there." He pointed to the row of orange plastic chairs in the waiting area.

Bea gave in reluctantly. "But you'd better tell us how he's doing just as soon as you've finished examining him!" She wagged a warning finger at him, and a passing nurse chuckled.

As the double doors swung closed behind the doctor and his patient, Lucy sank down in one of the hard chairs with a sigh of relief. At least Bea hadn't regaled the doctor with her version of how "David" had come to them. Of course, that didn't mean she still wouldn't.

But as her great-aunt sat down beside her, anxiety inevitably overwhelmed her. How many worried people had sat in this stark waiting room, with its yellowed linoleum floor, and felt this same anxiety? Despite herself, she wondered if he really would be all right.

But what could possibly happen to him now? she asked herself impatiently. He would recover his memory and go back to his normal life.

After all, she wasn't abandoning him. Here, there were doctors and nurses and other patients to keep him company. There was also more for him to do, and certainly he would receive more expert care than she and Bea could give him. And besides, he was *not* her responsibility.

After what seemed like hours spent flipping through ancient magazines, Dr. Marshall reemerged through the swinging doors.

"You can come in now."

He led them to an examination room where David was sitting on the edge of the bed, fully dressed.

Against the cream-colored Aran-knit sweater, his

hair looked very gold and his eyes very blue, even under the dismal fluorescent lights of the hospital.

Bea rushed to him and anxiously looked him over, brushing back a stray lock of golden brown hair from the fresh dressing on his forehead while he gave her an amused look. But when his gaze slipped over to Lucy, his expression became grave again.

The doctor clipped a head X ray to the lighted screen on the wall and Lucy was glad to have something else to focus on.

"Obviously Mr.—um—*David*, has been in some kind of accident. But there are no fractures, as you can see." He pointed to the ghostly image of the skull. "The contusion doesn't look too serious, and that's probably what's caused the amnesia. I expect it will be only temporary. Chances are, there'll be no long-term effects."

He flicked off the X-ray screen. "He just needs to take it easy for a few days and let nature take its course."

"Exactly what I would have said." Bea gave Doc Marshall a smug look. Then as he hurried off to his next patient, she turned to their guest. "You'll come back home with us, of course, and rest there."

Lucy bit her lip in dismay. She should have foreseen this.

David smiled, but shook his head. "Oh, no, I can't possibly do that. I've been enough trouble to you and Lucy already. I'll stay at a hotel here in town."

Bea's eyebrows rose in two fine arcs. "Oh, so my B and B isn't good enough for you? I'll have you know you won't find better, or cheaper, accommodation in this county."

His smile broadened into a grin that gave Lucy a disturbing quiver, but he shook his head. "You know it's not that."

"Then what is it?" Bea looked perplexed.

Clearly at a loss for an answer, he turned his gaze to Lucy, with a look of appeal in his eyes.

Who could blame the man for not wanting to go back to the crazy setup he'd just escaped? She rushed in to help. "Bea, perhaps David would rather stay in town, where he wouldn't be so isolated—"

"Isolated! You talk as if we were stuck in the wilderness. I won't hear another argument. It's settled. He's staying."

Lucy looked at David with a little shrug. There was no point in arguing with her great-aunt.

"I'll stay on one condition," he said firmly. "You let me pay my way and do my share of the work."

"That's two conditions," Bea objected. "And it's not our usual practice to put our guests to work."

"That's okay. I'm not your usual kind of guest."

That was for sure!

He looked at Bea gravely. "Until I know who I am, I have no money. It's the only way I can compensate you for my keep."

"Who said anything about compensation!" Bea looked quite put out. "If you really want to compensate, stop arguing with me."

He grinned, then sobered. "Shouldn't we ask Lucy how she feels about this?" His gaze slid over to her, suddenly enigmatic.

Here was her chance to make her wishes known, but suddenly the words wouldn't come out.

Bea jumped in and saved her. "Whatever for?"

"She may have had her fill of nursing an invalid,"

David stated wryly. Although he spoke to Bea, his gaze remained on her.

"There hasn't been much nursing to do. You're far too independent to make a good invalid. And I hope she's much too shrewd a businesswoman to turn away good trade, or I haven't taught her right."

Lucy gave him a weak smile. "Of course. You must stay."

Was she reluctant, or stupidly glad to have him? Both, she decided, and that was the trouble.

WHEN THEY LEFT the hospital he was glad to climb into the passenger seat of the Honda, and glad of the dark glasses protecting his eyes from the dazzling snow that covered everything.

The painkillers he'd been prescribed had already worked wonders. A dull residual ache was all that remained, thank God. And hearing the doctor confirm that he was in pretty good shape made him feel even better.

As they headed for the small police station in town, he looked curiously at the main street of Hazeldene. It was more a village, really, he thought as they drove the short distance and parked next to a mountain of snow piled on the curb.

Within two blocks he'd seen most of the amenities any town needed, including a supermarket, a post office and a small library. The police station was housed in the lower part of the town hall, which also seemed to be used as a summer theater. And he noticed the fire station just down one of the side streets.

It was a nice, compact, friendly-looking little town. He liked it, even though it was profoundly disorienting not to have memories of other places to compare it to. Was he from a small town? Was that why he felt so at home here?

Even the police station had a casual, neighborly feel. A burly old sergeant in rolled-up shirtsleeves stood behind the counter, greeting Bea and Lucy with a friendly smile. He listened sympathetically while they explained his plight.

Filing his own missing-persons report gave him the oddest feeling. After all, *he* knew where he was; it was his whole world that was missing.

They took his picture, and he let them have his fingerprints, too, although it made him think uneasily about that strange scar on his shoulder, and the one just like it that Doc Marshall had found on his back. It looked like a bullet wound, he'd said.

Bullet wound? What kind of man was he? What if he had a criminal record?

Finally, the sergeant stacked the completed forms and stapled them together. "Like I said, we haven't heard about any accidents that might explain what happened to you, but I'll get this out on the wire. You can be sure we'll call you at Miss Bea's as soon as we get any information.

"Don't worry, son." The old guy's businesslike manner dropped away and he gave David an encouraging smile. "We'll find out who you are and where you belong. But for now, you couldn't be in a better spot than Miss Bea's."

Then he turned to Lucy, and his smile became teasing. "Blaine will be sorry he missed you, Lucy. He had to head over to Witchwood this morning. Some nut at the doughnut shop said he'd been transported there against his will."

Beside him, Bea gave a little indrawn gasp, and he saw her exchange a guilty look with Lucy. But David hardly noticed.

Blaine? Who was Blaine? And why did he suddenly feel so tense and annoyed?

The officer chuckled and shook his head. "Ten to one this guy escaped from some loony bin."

"Oh, I certainly hope so," Bea muttered fervently.

"By the way, Lucy," the sergeant continued. "I guess the class is canceled tonight, with the weather and all. More snow coming our way."

She nodded distractedly. "Yes, I'm afraid so. I'll call everyone and let them know we'll have to start up next week instead. So how's your quilt coming along? Did you get much done over the holidays?"

He leaned one massive, hairy forearm on the counter, and said confidentially to Lucy, "I've been having a heck of a time with that Folded Star square."

"Oh, aren't they a pain? Well, bring it along to the next class and we'll see what the problem is."

David shook his head. That settled it, he *was* still in la-la land.

As they emerged onto the snow-covered sidewalk, Bea did a swift right turn, away from where the car was parked, and headed down the street.

"Come along, you two." All business, she trotted ahead in her sturdy little snow-boots. "Lunch, and then we have to get you some clothes."

After a quick and somewhat-uncomfortable lunch at the town diner, they followed Bea down the street once again. Suddenly she turned abruptly and disappeared into the doorway of a store.

He grinned. She was like some kind of ancient pixie in her fur-trimmed, hooded coat. She certainly didn't walk like any old person he ever knew. Catching himself, he shook his head. Did he know any other old people?

Following her into the store, he held the door open for Lucy, who walked silently beside him. Ever since they had arrived at the hospital she'd been quiet and withdrawn. It didn't take a genius to see she was troubled by the latest turn of events.

For her sake, he should decline Bea's generous offer. But Lucy was also precisely the reason why he wanted to accept it.

He sensed she needed to talk to someone. There was something she was afraid of, something keeping her from finding love in her life, and he was curious to learn what that was and help her overcome it, if he could.

Lucy was too vital and caring a woman to live without love. And that was the only reason he wanted to stay. That, and the fact that she gave him something else to think about other than his own problem.

"Good morning, Frank."

Bea's brisk voice brought him out of his reverie. He glanced around and noticed he was in a men's clothing store, and that the clerk was approaching them from the counter at the back.

"Miss Bea! Lucy! What a nice surprise."

For some reason, David didn't like the insinuating sound of the man's voice.

"Hello, Frank," Lucy said tonelessly.

"So good to see you, Lucy." The hungry look the clerk turned on Lucy made him want to push the guy's face in.

Obviously he had violent tendencies, but that didn't bother him right now. This guy did.

Was it something about his slick, phony look? Or was it the voracious expression in his eyes when they rested on Lucy?

Beside him, he sensed Lucy's tension. Was it just his imagination, or had she moved a little closer to his side? He fought the urge to put his arm around her shoulders and pull her against him.

"What can I do for you?" Frank bared his teeth in a slow smile.

"What do think?" Bea replied, with a touch of asperity. "You can sell us some clothes."

"Well, you know we only sell men's clothes." Frank patted the stack of shirts on the table beside him, a condescending smile on his thin lips.

David had an overwhelming desire to wipe that smile off his ferretlike face.

"What a coincidence, because that's what I want to buy." Bea turned her back to Frank and rolled her eyes heavenward.

He smothered a grin. Whether he was the kind of man who made snap judgments or not didn't matter. It was obvious Bea didn't like the guy, either. And he could see why.

"Now, let me see, we'll need a couple of pairs of pants," Bea continued. "Brushed cotton twill is nice and warm for winter. Do you have anything like that?"

Lucy jumped in. "Bea, why don't we just let...David browse around and pick out what he needs."

He tried to catch her eye, but she refused to look at him. He felt a stab of disappointment.

Lucy then led Bea to a wooden chair beside the dressing room, and went to gaze out the plate-glass door at the street scene.

He flipped through a rack of pants, not paying much attention to the selection.

Frank had strolled over to Lucy, and now stood far too close to her. "So, how have you been?" His oily voice dropped to a low, intimate tone.

"Fine," she said with a tense smile, and edged imperceptibly backward.

He realized that he was squeezing a fistful of fabric in his hand. He let go of the crumpled pants and continued to sort through the rack, trying not to pay attention.

"Listen, Lucy," Frank continued. "If you're free, the Valentine's Dance is coming up. I thought we could go together."

"I'm sorry, Frank." She shook her head, and David felt relieved. Good, she wasn't going out with that reptile in a suit.

"I have a date already," she continued, and his relief turned to staggering bitterness. Who with? Blaine?

"Oh!" Frank's pitying look suggested that it was her loss. "Well, how about some other evening, whenever you're free?"

"I'll let you know."

"Young man, don't bother chatting up my niece." Bea's penetrating voice carried clearly across the store. "You already had your chance with her, and you seem to have blown it. Now, get on with your work and help my friend find some clothes."

Frank flushed a dark brick red and shot Bea a resentful look. "Excuse me, Lucy." He stalked over to stand on the other side of the rack and stared at him with veiled disdain. "Can I help you with anything? What size are you looking for?"

But his attention was on Lucy, who continued to gaze out onto the main street, oblivious to what was happening in the store behind her. He felt the urge to get her away from this creep.

For her sake, he hurriedly chose the minimum quantity of clothes. Bea paid, although he hated to see her hand over her credit card. He wouldn't rest until he'd paid her back.

Pulling off the tags, he slipped on the new navy parka and picked up the shopping bag of clothing from the counter, stowing the borrowed topcoat inside it.

As soon as they got out of the store, Lucy turned on Bea. "I don't care much for Frank, either, but you shouldn't have embarrassed him like that."

Bea snorted. "He deserves to be embarrassed. You said yourself he was a loathsome octopus with the sensitivity of topsoil...."

Lucy's cheeks flamed the same bright red as her woolen hat. "Do you have to repeat everything I say? Besides, that was different...."

Bea waved away her protest as she trotted back toward the car. "Oh, Lucy, lighten up. That man is a conceited oaf who tries my patience." She turned to him. "Lucy dated him once. It was a real disaster. But in a town this size there's not much to choose from. That's why we had to call for you."

She made it sound so utterly logical. He glanced over at Lucy, but she refused to look his way. So why was he so damn glad that Frank had obviously failed to win her favor?

Now, more than ever, he wanted to know what made Lucy tick.

WHEN THEY REACHED the car, he insisted on giving up the front seat to Bea. It was a tough fight, but he finally won, much to Lucy's relief. Having him sit beside her in the tiny Honda would have been torture.

David helped Bea get over the snowbank edging the sidewalk and into the passenger seat, then climbed in the back.

As Lucy settled behind the wheel and fastened her seat belt, she looked up into the rearview mirror and caught sight of his dark glasses. Was he looking at her? That vulnerable feeling swamped her again. Oh, no. This was worse, much worse.

"You must be tired, David." Bea turned and shot him an astute look over her shoulder. "I think you've been up and about long enough."

She was right, Lucy thought, glancing at him in the mirror again. He did look pale.

As she started up the engine, Bea said comfortingly, "It'll be nice to get home. I'll make you a good hot meal. We'll eat in front of the fire, and have a nice relaxing evening."

Lucy shivered with trepidation. It sounded too cozy, too intimate and much too appealing. She didn't know whether she felt excited or terrified.

As she drove down King Street and on out of town, she noticed that it seemed very dark for early afternoon, even in the depths of January. To the west, a charcoal-gray sky hung low and threatening. It looked as if another storm was heading their way.

How long would this one last? How long could she endure these crazy feelings of yearning? Even if they found out who he was tomorrow, it might be days before he could finally leave.

She shivered, suddenly feeling like a woman going to her doom.

7

As they turned off the road onto the tree-lined driveway, Lucy flicked the wipers up a notch. She could barely see the dark silhouette of the house up ahead through the blowing white veil. The light snow that had begun just as they had left town was already falling thicker and faster.

Panic made her hands tighten on the steering wheel. It was all very well and good, giving in to the forbidden secret desire to have him stay, but what was she hoping to get out of this? Why had she willfully ignored the myriad possibilities for disaster?

What if he was married? The thought hit her like a bombshell. At this very moment, some poor woman, somewhere, could be pacing the floor, worried sick, while she, Lucy, coveted her husband.

How could she not have considered the possibility before? What had she been thinking? She'd been thinking about satisfying her own carnal desires, and not much else. Casual sex with a passing stranger—how much lower could she sink?

Why hadn't she come to her senses before they'd left town? Anxiety returned, full force.

Lucy used to find the old brick house rather large and comfortable, but in the past few days it had shrunk to claustrophobic proportions. And it was only going to get worse. How was she going to manage being cooped up with him again, without him guessing her shameful feelings?

Pulling up by the front door, she turned to Bea. "You two go on in. I'll just be a few minutes," she said stiffly. "We'll need more wood before the weather closes in."

"All right, dear. I'll put the kettle on."

David had already gotten out and was opening Bea's door.

Lucy looked away as he bent down and helped her great-aunt out of the car. She just needed some time alone, away from him and the disturbing feelings he roused in her. Somehow, she had to stem the tide of panic welling up inside her. Wasn't she a strong, independent woman who met life head-on? At least, that was what she'd always assumed about herself. Now she was beginning to wonder. In any case, she had to keep her perspective when it came to this stranger.

After turning the car around in the cleared area in front of the garage, she backed inside and turned off the engine. She got out of the car, slamming the door a little harder than necessary.

At worst, she only had to cope for another couple of days. Surely the police would come up with something by then. And of course, his memory would probably be restored soon. Dr. Marshall had said it was only temporary.

A gust of cold wind froze her face as she emerged from the garage. She struggled to close the large wooden door, pushing against the blast, but it blew so hard, even standing upright was difficult.

Suddenly a black-gloved hand appeared above her own against the faded blue door. She turned and squinted into the driving snow to see him there beside her.

With his help, the door moved easily into place. He pushed down the wooden latch, and it was secure.

A warm quiver worked its way up her body. She didn't feel cold anymore; she burned with a savage heat that had her trembling.

Turning abruptly, she ducked her head against the icy blast of the storm and headed around the corner of the garage toward the lean-to where they kept the wood.

Struggling to keep her footing, she hung on to the garage wall with one hand as she fought against the freezing wind pushing her back and stinging her face with snow. She could scarcely breathe.

Was it just the wind, or her sense that he was close behind her, making her feel like a hunted thing, prey to her own uncontrollable emotions?

She reached the lean-to against the back wall of the garage, piled high with stacks of cordwood. Although open at both ends, it offered some kind of shelter and allowed her to catch her breath. But only for a moment.

He'd followed her, and now stood close beside her, his body brushing hers in the small space. Her heart beat too fast, and it became an effort to drag the icy air into her lungs.

"You shouldn't be out here. Go back to the house. I can manage this myself." Without looking up at him, she began to take logs from the top of the pile.

"I know you can, but I'm helping anyway!" He had to yell to be heard above the fury of the wind, but the determination in his voice was unmistakable.

She glanced up at him and wished she hadn't. She

felt intensely self-conscious under his steady gaze. "You heard the doctor. You have to take it easy."

"Carrying a few logs won't hurt me." His arms were full already and he stood waiting for her, watching her. But when she had finally loaded up, he made no move to leave, just stood blocking the way, looking down at her with a grave expression in his eyes.

"Lucy, it's not too late." His voice was quieter now, yet seemed to cut through the howl of the wind around the fragile shelter. "If you don't want me here, I can go back to town."

Talk about putting her on the spot. She evaded the question. "This is a hell of a place to have a conversation."

"It's the only place we can be alone to discuss this." He moved a little closer, his breath clouding in the frigid air. "We both know what Bea wants for us."

Yes, but it wasn't what Bea wanted that worried her so much; it was her own desire that scared her to death. And if he knew how she felt, he would be scared, too. No doubt romance was the last thing on his mind.

"How would you get back to town, anyway?"

Beneath the hood of his parka, his expression remained serious. "I'd walk."

"Yeah, right." She gave him a skeptical look.

"It's not that far and if I stuck to the road I wouldn't get lost."

"No, you'd just freeze to death."

"Not in my new coat. If you want me to leave, I will. Do you want me to leave, Lucy?"

Now was her chance. Despite Bea's offer, she knew somehow that he would do whatever she said. She just had to speak the truth. What did she want?

She shook her head slightly. "No, I don't want you to leave. I wouldn't send you out there to take your chances. What kind of a person do you think I am?" But that wasn't the only reason, or even the main one.

"The question is, what kind of person do you think *I* am? I know I make you uncomfortable, and I can't say I blame you. After all, you know nothing about me." Under the hood, his blue eyes were troubled. "I had no coat on, no identification on me. Perhaps there *was* a breakout at the asylum that night. Me and the nutcase at the doughnut shop..."

"Are you trying to tell me you think you're insane?" she asked.

He shrugged. "Who knows? I could be."

He looked so grave that for a moment she wasn't quite sure what to say. Once again, the enormity of his loss slammed into her. She could barely imagine how frightening it must be, to know nothing about oneself.

"I don't think so. And I don't have any fears for our safety." That, at least, was the absolute truth.

For a long moment his gaze ran over her face, and for once she could actually meet it. Then a smile curved the corners of his mouth. The warmth in his eyes seemed to reach right down inside her, and she had to look away again.

"Thank you," he said. "That means a lot."

"Be honest. You couldn't make it into town right now, could you?"

He looked uncomfortable for a moment, then finally gave a rueful shake of his head.

She stared up at him in amazement. "And yet, you would have gone if I'd asked you to?"

He nodded. "Yes."

"Why?"

"Because it's the least I could do after everything you've done for me," he said simply.

Looking up into his eyes, she saw warmth and gratitude, and something else. Something that made her pulse quicken.

The wind roared and howled outside the fragile shelter, and they might have been a million miles from anywhere. All alone. Suddenly, with breathtaking urgency, she wanted to be in his arms, she wanted him to kiss her, to possess her right there. The need was so acute, she could almost taste his lips.

Her knees threatened to buckle, and a melting sensation spread through every inch of her. Panic-stricken, she turned abruptly away and headed out the other side of the woodshed, oblivious to the force of the storm. It was the long way back to the house, but she didn't care. Bent against the wind, she stumbled through the snow and finally kicked on the screen door with her boot. David was just behind her. A moment later, Bea opened up.

Propping the door ajar with her shoulder, Lucy jerked her head toward the interior. "Go ahead," she said to him tersely.

She let him walk past her, into the mudroom at the back of the kitchen, before stepping inside and letting the door slam shut behind her.

"We'll need more than that, Lucy." Her great-aunt eyed the loads they carried.

"Yes, I know." She took the logs over to the far corner, squatted down, and dropped them on the floor.

He did the same and began stacking the wood beside hers.

She turned to him with what she hoped was brisk detachment. "I can manage the rest on my own."

"But you'll get it done quicker with my help. C'mon, we're wasting time and the storm is getting worse." He stood and smiled down at her, then turned and went out again.

That look sent another shiver of panic racing through her. Had she given herself away?

As she followed him out the door, she caught Bea's sly grin of pleasure. Naturally, Bea had noticed, and naturally she was drawing the wildest conclusions. The problem was, they weren't so wild. With a groan of frustration, Lucy banged the door shut behind her. Talk about being caught between a rock and a hard place.

AFTER BRINGING IN the last load, he hung up his snow-caked coat beside Lucy's and left his boots next to hers in the mudroom.

As he followed her into the welcome warmth of the spacious kitchen, he breathed in a spicy fragrance that filled the air. Under the dark, beamed ceiling, Bea was standing by the stove, ladling something red and steaming into old pewter mugs.

"This will warm you up." She handed one to each of them.

Lucy took a sip, then frowned down at the liquid in the mug. "What's wrong with this cider?" She sniffed it cautiously.

"There's nothing wrong with it," Bea said offhandedly.

"Have you tried it?" Lucy persisted. "It doesn't taste like your usual mulled cider."

Bea shot her an annoyed, impatient look. "Well, it is. Just drink it."

Giving her great-aunt a suspicious frown, Lucy put her mug down on the kitchen counter.

He took a cautious sip. Among the rich flavors of apple, cinnamon and nutmeg there was an odd hint of something different, something unexpected, but it wasn't unpleasant. And of course, he didn't know what Bea's usual cider tasted like.

Besides, he was cold to the bone, and this was warming him up from the inside out. He drained the mug as Bea watched him closely, her head cocked to one side like an alert little sparrow. When he put it down on the kitchen counter, she had a small, satisfied smile on her face.

"See, Lucy, David has finished all his cider. Why don't you do the same?" She shot her niece a sly, sideways glance from her blue eyes.

Lucy put her hands on her hips and leveled her with an uncompromising look. "Out with it, Bea. What are you up to now?"

For once, her irrepressible great-aunt looked surprised. After a moment's silence, she soon collected her wits. "Lucy, do you really want to discuss it here and now?" She cocked her head toward him with a significant glance.

"You don't need to be so subtle," Lucy said dryly. "I told David all about the events leading up to his appearance."

Her great-aunt's face split into an approving smile. "Now that's showing some gumption, my girl, and not a moment too soon. You see, I've been thinking about that man in Witchwood. What if he's the one who was meant, and David *did* end up here by accident?" Her gaze flashed over him with a smile, her eyes dancing with warmth and affection. "But you're so perfect. It's *you* we want."

His heart leaped at Bea's words.

Down, boy. Was he crazy, wanting Lucy to want him?

"That's why I've decided to leave nothing to chance." Bea picked up Lucy's mug, almost full and still steaming, and held it out to her. "Now drink your cider."

"Maybe later," Lucy replied dubiously.

"Just finish it off for now," her great-aunt urged again. "To be on the safe side."

"At this point, I don't need any more supernatural interference." Lucy waved it away.

That gave him his answer. He was crazy. Why on earth would she want *him* around? A man with no past and an uncertain future. After all, what if this memory loss wasn't temporary?

Bea's mouth compressed with impatience. "Oh, well, at least you had one sip, and sometimes one sip is all it takes. Now, come along, David." She moved toward the doorway and beckoned him with a crooked finger. "I've made up the Parrot Room for you. Now that you're mobile, I'm sure you'd be more comfortable in a real bed."

"The Parrot Room. Sounds like a nightclub." He grinned, trying to subdue his lingering sense of dissatisfaction. Despite her assurance that he was welcome, he could see that Lucy still felt uncomfortable around him.

"It was Georgie's room." Bea gave a distant little smile. "It's the wallpaper, you know."

He didn't, but he was sure he would soon find out. He followed Bea out of the kitchen into the broad entry hall.

"But why the Parrot Room?" Lucy rushed past him and blocked Bea's way. He could hear the knife edge of panic in her voice. "Do you think that's a good idea? He might find it a little overwhelming."

"Overwhelming! It'll be stimulating. That's what he needs to jog that memory—stimulation!"

"But you never rent Uncle Georgie's room to strangers," Lucy protested anxiously.

"Lucy, David is no stranger," Bea said decisively, pushing her out of the way and hurrying up the wide staircase with Lucy at her heels.

He paused on the first step. "Actually, Bea, I am a stranger, as much to myself as to you."

So why should Lucy trust him?

Bea made an impatient noise as she stopped and looked back. "Nonsense. I feel like I've known you forever. I just have to look into your eyes to see into your soul. Oh, yes, I know you very well."

Fortunately she didn't know everything. What would Bea think of the throbbing desire that had taken hold of him—this burning need to touch Lucy, to hold her, to make love with her? But he mustn't think about it; he had to fight it with everything he had.

"Besides—" Bea flapped her hand at him as she went on up the stairs "—I really don't think the powers-that-be would send a rascal, do you?"

He caught up with her on the landing. Dim light filtered through a large stained-glass window, bathing the gracious old stairway in jewel colors as he looked down at her ruefully.

"I have no idea. On the other hand there's the old saying, 'Be careful what you wish for.' Do you remember 'The Monkey's Paw'?"

Just above him, Lucy paused, her hand on the gleaming wood banister. She gave him a searching look. "You obviously do."

He must. But when he searched his mind for another connected thought, all he could come up with was a frustrating blank.

He shook his head in annoyance. "No, I don't remember anything else."

"Well, at least we know you're well-read," Lucy said dryly, as they reached the second floor and headed down the wide hallway.

"And obviously you are, too," he said quietly.

He looked around him with interest. On one side, the stairs dropped away below a wooden railing. On the other, a series of doors ranged down the hallway. Old prints and watercolors decorated the walls, and the carved moldings and gleaming wood of the beautiful old house continued in the upper story. At the end of the hall, a steep, narrow staircase led up to what must be the attic.

There was something about this house that seemed so familiar. He felt at home here.

"That's Lucy's room." Bea pointed to a door as they passed it.

"And where's your room?" he asked Bea.

"Down at the other end." She gestured vaguely, before throwing open the door next to Lucy's with a flourish. "Voilà!" She beamed up at him.

Lucy watched as he stepped inside and looked around, waiting for his reaction.

He slowly scanned the room with a look of growing incredulity on his lean, unshaven face.

"Uh... Wow," he finally said, slightly dazed.

That was an understatement.

In the softly-lit room, on all four walls, parrots of every possible color peeped from a wallpaper jungle of green foliage.

Suddenly his face paled. He put a hand to his forehead and swayed on his feet.

Immediately Lucy was at his side, gripping his elbow. "What's the matter? Are you dizzy again?"

"Do you feel weak?" Bea piped in with a worried frown. "Why don't you lie down, dear boy."

"No..." He shook his head and gently pulled his arm from her grasp. "No, I'm all right. It's just...another one of those images."

"Did you remember something else?" Lucy hovered anxiously at his side.

"I...I'm not sure." He frowned, trying to recall more.

"What is it? Just tell us."

"I just had this flash of a jungle. Fire and thick black smoke. People running..." The furrow between his brows deepened. "But I can't imagine what that could have to do with my life."

"Sounds like a scene from *Apocalypse Now*," Lucy suggested, trying to shrug off her unease. "Maybe you're just remembering a movie. And yet... There's your scar. Do you remember how you came by that?"

He thought for a moment, then shook his head.

She examined his face anxiously, but he cleared his expression and shot her a brilliant smile.

"Don't worry about it, Lucy. You've worried about me quite enough." With that, he moved farther into the room, looking around with genuine interest as Bea plumped cushions and straightened pictures that were already perfectly aligned.

She didn't believe for a moment that his worries didn't weigh on him, but it was obvious he didn't want to burden them. Once again she admired the strength that took. In his place she would be frantic and scared, and probably incapable of doing anything but dwelling on her predicament.

He went over to the big bow window overlooking the back garden and moved aside the lace curtains that hung beneath heavy moss green velvet swags. After briefly looking out on the drearily familiar sight of swirling snow, he turned back to examine the rest of the room.

The walls were hung with framed theater posters from Georgie Weston's triumphant days as a head-liner, and glamorous black-and-white photos of elegant and mysterious women. All Uncle Georgie, of course. And every lamp had a little square of pink silk hung over it. "Kinder to the complexion," she remembered him telling her in his gentle, whispery voice.

She smiled. Dear Uncle Georgie. He'd never minded the little girl exploring through his boxes and trunks, playing dress-up with his gorgeous costumes and finding treasures in his extravagant jewelry.

It was the kind of room she'd imagined for an old-time movie star. Ava Gardner, or someone like that.

Of course, he'd done Ava Gardner, too. To perfection.

With his hands on his narrow hips, David examined one of the portraits on the wall.

"You see," she said dryly. "I wasn't exaggerating. Perhaps you'd be more comfortable in one of the guest rooms."

He turned and looked at her with a gleam in his eyes, which she knew instinctively had nothing to do with being overwhelmed by the room. For no good reason at all, she was positive that he knew exactly how much it bothered her to have him sleeping right next door.

The heat rushed to her cheeks. She hated that he could make her feel so transparent.

"It's too late. I've already prepared this one," Bea said, giving her a stern glare. "Lucy, you're being very inhospitable and making David feel unwanted."

Unwanted? That was the problem—if only he was unwanted. She tried not to look in the direction of the bed. The carved four-poster was as extravagant as the rest of the room, hung with more filmy lace and freshly made up with a fluffy down comforter.

"It's all the same to me," he replied. "I'll stay wherever it's most convenient for you."

"Fine. You can stay right here," Bea stated flatly.

Lucy sighed in resignation. Bea could connive to her heart's content. All she had to do was keep a grip on reality, and on her wayward feelings.

She'd been waiting for some sign of derision from him, but there was none. Here he was, in this crazy, overblown room, looking at Georgie's mementos with a quiet smile of appreciation that moved her in the strangest way.

Her glance went to Bea, who was watching him with

a fondness that worried her. She'd taken this man to her heart, without reservation. She would be so hurt when nothing came of her grand scheme and he left to go back to his life.

Just then, Bea gave a deep sigh of contentment and softly clapped her hands. "Now, David, you have a little relax. I'm going downstairs to attend to dinner."

"Do you need any help?" Lucy asked swiftly, jumping at the chance to keep busy.

Bea shook her head decisively. "No, no. I have a casserole in the oven. Why don't you make sure David has everything he needs?"

Lucy sighed in defeat. "Sure." There was no point in arguing.

"Dinner will be ready in no time," her great-aunt said airily as she disappeared out the door.

As Bea's footsteps went pattering down the stairs, she turned to find him watching her with the quiet patience she found so nerve-racking.

"It looks like Bea has left you everything you need." She nodded toward the stack of towels on the cedar chest at the foot of the bed. "There are more towels in the bathroom, and you'll find fresh razors and toothbrushes in the cupboard under the sink. Now, if you don't mind, I've got work to do. I'll see you at dinner."

She turned on her heel and practically ran for the attic stairs.

Work, huh! She sat down at her desk, jumped up again and began pacing the floorboards, peering out at the snow every time she passed a window. She could barely think straight, let alone work.

It was perfectly understandable, wasn't it? Classic, even! These inexplicable feelings he stirred, this electrical attraction that drew her to him like—like some kind of magnet—well, there was no mystery about it, nothing supernatural. They were strangers trapped together by the storm. He was the grateful patient, she the nurse. It was a painfully typical, B-movie kind of situation.

But rationalizing didn't help one bit. He would be sleeping right next door!

If only it was just sex. Pure desire would be easier to dismiss, or at least keep under control. But it was his quiet humor, his affection for Bea, the gentle strength about him, and the direct, open look in his eyes.

Okay, so it was hard not to like him, but she would be a fool to go any further than that.

Except... She heaved a sigh and leaned her hands on the back of her chair. Except that whenever he was near, she felt drawn to him, as if she were singing inside. He made her want to get out and explore. He made her crave excitement. He made her feel like nothing she'd ever felt before. Like... *Magic.*

There was a soft knock at the door. She turned her head, and her heart leaped against her ribs. Suddenly it became hard to breathe. He was standing at the top of the stairs in the open doorway, watching her.

A terrifying electricity sprang up between them— the jolt of current so strong, so overwhelming, she couldn't believe he didn't feel it, too. The very air seemed to crackle and buzz with tension.

"I don't mean to intrude," he began diffidently. His blue eyes were shadowed and serious. "I want you to know that I appreciate the awkwardness of your situation, sleeping next door to a virtual stranger...." He let out a deep breath. "The point is, you don't have to hide from me, or feel like a prisoner in your own house."

"I don't." He wasn't the threat. Her own feelings were the enemy of them both.

"Then why are you up here pacing the floor?"

"I always pace when I'm working."

He looked a little skeptical. "Really?"

"Really." But she found it very difficult to meet his gaze. How could she, without revealing the truth? "It's true, I've been a little freaked out by the ordeal, and Bea's eccentricity isn't easy to cope with right now, but I'm not afraid of you."

He moved into the room with that surefooted, quiet confidence she found so unsettling, and stopped a couple of feet away on the bare pine boards. Despite herself, a ripple of tension tightened her muscles, but he made no move to come any closer.

"We both know the reality of our situation, even if Bea chooses to believe otherwise. I'll soon be gone, and your life will go back to normal."

"Yes," she said faintly.

"It would be irresponsible to act on any feelings that might grow out of these unusual circumstances that have brought us together."

What was he saying? That she'd somehow given herself away? That he sensed her attraction, and that it was mutual? Her breathing became quick and shallow as excitement and fear curled inside her.

"There's no question about that." She tried—and failed—to sound emphatic.

A faint smile played around his mouth. "Then that makes it easier. We're both in perfect agreement. We have nothing to worry about."

Suddenly they were plunged into total darkness.

Lucy gave a startled squeak and instinctively reached for him. Her fingers met ribbed wool, and felt the contours of his chest. The next moment his hands curved reassuringly around her arms and pulled her close.

For a second, she was clinging to him. His arms tightened around her, and then she felt his warm lips on hers. She wasn't sure who moved toward whom— only that they collided with an inexorable force.

Sensation exploded through her unlike anything she'd ever experienced before—a greedy, mindless fervor, a burning need to taste him, to breathe him in, to pour her hunger into him. He kissed her back with an urgency that told her how much he wanted this, too, as if they had both been starving for it all their lives. His arms wrapped around her like steel bands, holding her tightly.

A moment later, the lights came on again. They jerked apart, chests heaving.

He stared at her incredulously, and she could only imagine the look of shock on her own face. What had happened? That wasn't just a kiss! That was some kind of nuclear meltdown.

"David, Lucy, are you all right?"

At the sound of Bea's voice from the lower hallway, they sprang farther apart.

"Yes... Yes, we're fine, Bea." Her voice wobbled and fluttered; it was the best she could manage.

"C'mon down. Dinner's ready."

"Be right there."

Oh, no. She couldn't face her great-aunt just yet. She could hardly bring herself to face David. It was insane to feel this depth of emotion, this wild riot of sensations under circumstances like these.

A faint flush edged his cheeks, and his chest still rose and fell rapidly. "Lucy, I never meant for that to happen."

She shook her head convulsively. "Me neither."

"The way things are, I have no business, no right feeling the way I do. And the way I feel..." He seemed to be struggling for words.

She cut in quickly. "It's just sexual attraction, compounded by the isolation and...and all these weird circumstances. I suppose it could happen to anyone."

"But it can't happen to us."

"Believe me, you don't have to remind me of that." After trying so hard to hide her reactions, she couldn't believe they were actually talking about this so frankly. Nevertheless, she had to say what had to be said. "For all we know, you could have a wife."

He slowly nodded. "I've thought of that, too. But if I am married, wouldn't she have reported my disappearance? Why isn't anybody looking for me?"

"I don't know." She only knew that if he were her husband, she would be worried out of her mind.

"The point is," he said soberly, "we can't act on these feelings again. That would be irresponsible."

"You're absolutely right." She let out a deep breath, with a rush of relief. "I want you to know that I don't normally act this way."

"You don't have to explain. I understand. We've been thrown together, or as Bea would have it, brought together by magic."

She groaned. "Not you, too."

He smiled. "No, I don't believe in hocus-pocus...although I have to admit it all seems very odd. By the way, what do you think Bea put in the cider?"

She rolled her eyes. "Who knows? Let's just hope it wasn't belladonna."

He let out a soft chuckle, then his expression became sober. "Magic aside, we've both been under a lot of stress. Something was bound to give."

"Lucy? David? Are you coming?"

Bea came pattering up the stairs and popped her head through the door. She had a red velvet scarf wrapped around her head like a turban, pinned with a rhinestone brooch, and was wearing the scarlet damask caftan she always referred to as her "best winter gown."

"I hope you weren't alarmed by the power failure. That happens from time to time, especially in bad weather. I was worried about you getting disoriented in the dark."

"I was fine." David moved to stand in front of Bea, and Lucy realized he'd done it to shield her from her great-aunt's prying eyes. She could just imagine what her expression revealed right now. "Shall we go downstairs?" He swept Bea ahead of him out of the room.

His thoughtfulness both touched and disturbed her. That kind of thing only made him more dangerously attractive.

Who was this man? Why did he make her feel this way?

Whatever this feeling for him might be, it wasn't going away. In fact, hour by hour, it just kept getting harder to cope with. And now that she knew the feeling was mutual...

Slowly, she followed them down the stairs. Pausing

for a moment on the bottom step, she touched a finger to her lips, still throbbing and tingling from his kiss.

God help her, she wanted more. And that was absolutely out of the question.

8

ALTHOUGH SHE TOOK a few minutes to compose herself, her legs were still trembling as she walked down the stairs, heading for the kitchen. When she reached the hall, she noticed that the dining-room door was open.

She walked toward the room and stopped dead on the threshold.

Oh, no.

There were glowing candles everywhere—in the old silver candelabras on the table, in the wrought-iron wall sconces, and on the mantel above the log fire.

Apart from being dressed for some kind of state occasion, Bea had clearly pulled out all the stops in an effort to make this a "special" dinner.

The soft light reflected from the beamed ceiling and gleamed off the lustrous old sideboard—obviously freshly polished. The table was laid with the very best silver, linen and crystal.

This was too romantic, too cozy—especially when she met David's eyes across the room. They held hers with a quietly burning intensity, but otherwise he seemed perfectly relaxed and in control.

If only she could feel that way! A tremor of fear made her stomach tighten. And yet in spite of her fear, the temptation to explore this all-consuming passion was too great to be ignored.

"Has something happened between you two? Something I should know about?" From her seat at the head of the table, Bea was watching Lucy with shrewd contemplation.

"What do you mean?" She winced. If only Bea would develop laryngitis. She shot her great-aunt a quelling look, but of course Bea paid it no attention, and turned her probing gaze on David.

"Come on, David. You're not as obtuse as my niece is pretending to be right now. You know what I mean."

"I'm afraid you've lost me, too." David returned Bea's scrutiny with a bland look, not betraying any guilty awareness.

He had a quality of stillness, like that of some powerful, graceful animal. He never fidgeted, wasn't restless, but was always strong and self-contained, as he was right now.

"Come, come. There's nothing to be embarrassed about." She began ladling rice from one of the casseroles in the center onto their plates. "Park yourself, Lucy." Bea pointed to the third place setting. "Dinner's getting cold."

David got up and held out a chair. Approaching reluctantly, Lucy lowered herself onto the red brocade seat. She kept her eyes fixed on the empty plate in front of her. If she didn't look at him, maybe she could handle this.

"After all, magic can only do so much." Bea resumed her persecution. "You have to give it a helping hand."

"Bea, please..." Lucy pressed her fingertips to her eyelids for a moment, trying to marshal her strength. "We've heard enough about magic and spells. Eccentricity apart, you're taking this thing too far."

"Who's eccentric?" Setting the spoon back in the rice, Bea sat up straighter and shot her an indignant look, as the red velvet turban wobbled a little. "A person would have to be blind not to see that the two of you have something brewing between you. If that isn't magic, what is it?"

"That's not the point," Lucy replied, hastily brushing the question aside. "You have no business embarrassing and manipulating a guest in your house like this!"

"I'm not trying to embarrass anyone." Bea was unperturbed. "I'm just trying to make you face what's happening. To accept that this was meant to be."

"Bea, you don't understand. David has left a life behind somewhere. A life that could include a wife, children..." She stopped, aghast. Yet another horrible possibility that hadn't occurred to her until now. With every moment, she became more and more conscious of how inappropriate this was, if not downright morally wrong. She had no business feeling this way about him. No business at all.

"Then why isn't someone looking for him?" Bea questioned.

"I don't know."

Suddenly a terrifying thought hit her. Her hand flew to her mouth to stifle a gasp of horror. What if the people who would miss him had been with him when the accident had occurred?

Her gaze darted over to David. He returned it steadily, then shook his head. "I don't think I had anyone with me."

"How can you know?" she asked anxiously.

He became lost in thought for a moment, then met

her gaze with serious eyes. "When I first came to, all I remembered was walking in the snow. And before that, I seemed to be trapped in some kind of cramped, dark space. I doubt I dreamed it, I've been thinking about it, and I must have been in some kind of car accident. I'm sure of one thing—I was all alone, because I remember thinking that if I didn't get myself out of there, I'd die."

A log snapped and popped in the fireplace, but Lucy paid it no attention. Her gaze was riveted to David's lean face, sculpted by the warm light.

"If I do have a wife and kids, they weren't with me."

And she believed him. No matter what condition he was in, she couldn't imagine David walking away from a person in need of his help.

"Then why haven't they reported your disappearance?" Bea asked triumphantly, giving them both a gloating smile.

Suddenly David grinned at her, a teasing glint in his eye. "Maybe I did away with them, stuffed them in the freezer and was running from the scene of the crime when I had the accident."

Bea snorted. "And maybe I'm the queen of Sheba! Did you kiss each other? Is that why you both looked so stricken when I came up?"

Lucy heaved an exasperated sigh. "Okay, yes. We kissed each other. Are you happy now?"

A buzzer went off in the kitchen. Bea jumped to her feet, crowing. "It worked! The love charm in the cider worked."

She headed out of the room, and Lucy could see her slipper-clad feet doing a little self-satisfied shuffle beneath the scarlet draperies of her caftan.

"Serve up the Beef Paprikash, Lucy," came a disembodied but triumphant voice from the hall.

Across the table she met David's warm, sympathetic gaze. He understood; he was her ally. That made her feel comforted, but didn't dispel the dangerous sexual awareness one bit.

A minute later Bea came back in and took her seat, smiling benevolently at each of them in turn. "Lucy, I hope this has made a believer of you, finally."

Lucy picked up the serving spoon and ladled Beef Paprikash onto her great-aunt's plate. "Your magic cider had nothing to do with anything. We've just been stuck in this damn house too long and everybody's acting strangely. You most of all!"

Bea ignored her and turned to David. "Are you attracted to my niece?"

Lucy gasped, but David didn't even blink.

His gaze shifted to her, and the warmth and admiration in his eyes made her breath catch in her throat. "I think your niece is a beautiful woman—kind and generous—"

"That's not answering my question," Bea persisted ruthlessly.

"You don't have to answer the question at all," Lucy interjected quickly, her voice tight.

He shook his head. "It's all right. I don't mind." He turned to Bea, his face serious. "Yes, I am very attracted to your niece. But I'm not free to feel that way. And I wouldn't hurt Lucy, or you, for the world."

Bea reached over and patted his hand. "Of course, you wouldn't. I have no fear of that. But you're already involved. Do you really think you can just walk away now, and pretend nothing has happened?"

"Nothing *has* happened," Lucy stated between clenched teeth. "As far as I'm concerned, he's just a stranger with a big problem. When he solves his problem, he'll be on his way. And now, can we please drop the subject?"

"If you insist," Bea said mildly, but Lucy knew that she hadn't given up; she was just retiring from the field—for the moment.

After dinner they went into the back parlor and settled down to play gin rummy. Lucy got out the cards from the drawer of the old rolltop desk. Bea sat down in the armchair near the glowing fire and carefully removed her turban.

Popping an intricately beaded green velvet fez onto her head—obligatory attire, as far as she was concerned—she settled down for the after-dinner ritual of smoking her hookah.

After giving the tall, exotic contraption a bemused look, David acted as if hookah-smoking old ladies were an everyday sight. He also seemed to remember the rules of the game they were playing. But Lucy was having trouble concentrating on the cards in her hand as she dealt another round.

Usually she found the gentle bubbling of the pipe, and the aromatic smoke relaxing, but tonight it only added to her anxiety by introducing an erotic, sultry note to the atmosphere—making her think of *Arabian Nights* and harems...and making love.

Every atom of her awareness focused on David, seated on the couch on the other side of the coffee table.

If only she could escape outdoors, where she usually went to work out her problems. But the wind continued shrieking down the chimney and around the house, and the constant sharp pattering of snow against the windows reminded her that she was a prisoner.

She tried not to look at him—that was too dangerous. But in spite of herself, she couldn't help stealing a glance under her lashes at his lean face, sculpted by the firelight. With a surge of yearning, she could still feel the firm warmth of his mouth on hers, remember the taste of him. And, God help her, she wanted all that again.

At ten o'clock, Bea tossed her cards on the table and stood. She stretched and yawned. "Well, I'm off to bed. Good night, kids."

"Good night, Bea." David had risen to his feet and towered over her great-aunt's small frame. To Lucy's surprise, he leaned down and placed a kiss on Bea's thin cheek.

With an adoring smile, she reached up and took his face between her hands. "I'm so very glad you came into our lives."

She let him go, turned to Lucy, and gave her a kiss on the cheek. "Good night, my love."

"Wait, I'll come with you."

Bea stopped and looked at her, one eyebrow cocked in surprise. "Why?"

"I might as well go to bed, too."

"At ten o'clock! What's the matter with you?" Her astonishment was genuine. "It's not like you to go to bed so early. Stay. Keep David company. Get to know each other. Stop running away from your destiny, Lucy."

Bea continued on out the door. As her footsteps on

the staircase died away, the silence closed in and tightened between them until it became unbearable.

Lucy finally lifted her gaze to find David giving her that quiet, unwavering look that seemed to penetrate her deepest secrets while giving nothing of his own away. But then, she had nothing to hide any longer, she reminded herself.

"I really think I *should* go to bed, too. The trouble is, I want to stay," she admitted.

"Then stay."

"I don't think that's a very good idea. Do you?"

His soft voice reached out to her again. "But I'd like to get to know you. I enjoy being with you, Lucy."

"I like being with you, too." She felt very shy as she suddenly realized how true that was.

"If you stay in that chair, and I stay here, we can't get into much trouble, can we?"

"One small coffee table isn't much protection."

"But my word that I won't cross it should be."

"It *would* be, if you were the one I couldn't trust," she said dryly.

He smiled. She sank into the chair she had just vacated and he returned to his seat on the chintz sofa. He sat back, his chin propped on his hand, his index finger resting against his firm mouth.

Her gaze lingered there a moment too long. She cleared her throat, acutely self-conscious. "So, what will we talk about?"

A warm twinkle lit his eyes. "You choose."

"Well, that's obvious. I'd like to know more about you. I wonder what you do. It can't be anything mundane, like an accountant, or bank manager. It just doesn't fit." With his physical toughness, he seemed more like a man of action than someone who spent his days behind a desk.

She suppressed an impatient sigh. This was crazy. She was romanticizing him again. There was nothing romantic about the problem he faced. "You must be very worried," she said.

"Not so much worried as confused by these random images that keep popping into my head. And this dream I keep having."

"What dream?" She looked at him curiously, glad to find a safer topic than their mutual attraction.

But he seemed reluctant to say more. "Listen, I think you've coped with enough. You don't need me dumping on you. I can handle this."

"Tell me about it," she persisted. It couldn't be healthy for him to keep his anxieties bottled up.

He was quiet for a long time, until she thought he wasn't going to answer. "The dream itself is quite innocuous," he said finally, but there was a troubled crease in his brow, and he was looking far into the distance. "Nothing actually happens. It's the feeling it gives me of something horrible waiting in the wings."

"But you don't know what?"

"No. But I have a terrible suspicion that it's something awful that I was going to, or running from, when the accident happened. I wonder what I've done." His gaze met hers and she saw fear and helplessness in his eyes that struck a chord. "Dr. Marshall says the scar on my chest could have been caused by a bullet."

Bullet? A jolt of alarm quickly gave way to the overpowering urge to reassure him. "I don't think you're capable of doing something awful." She spoke with conviction. He had a goodness about him; she could feel it in his touch, see it in his eyes.

He pinned her with a sober look. "It's very sweet of you to have so much faith in me, but neither you nor I can know that, for sure."

She couldn't argue with that, but in her heart she couldn't believe it. "I don't like to see you so troubled. I wish I could make the pain go away."

He held her gaze, and once again that hot, dangerous awareness flowed through her and filled the space between them.

"And you could, but we can't." His blue eyes darkened as he slowly scrutinized her. "Believe me, if I were only following my own inclinations, I'd be over there right now making love with you."

A rush of aching need swept through her, making her shudder. She held out a hand as if to ward him off, although he hadn't moved.

"I just don't understand this, any of it," she said breathlessly. "Nothing like it has ever happened to me before. It's almost as if it were—" She searched for the right word to describe this force that had struck her out of the blue and demolished her reason.

"—Supernatural?" He completed the sentence for her.

She nodded helplessly. "If one were inclined to superstition, which I'm not. At least, I never thought I was—until now," she finished gloomily. "Over and over I've asked myself, why is this happening to me? And why you? Why not—"

"Blaine?" he interrupted quietly. When she paused he continued, "Who is Blaine?"

She could only stare at him. "A friend."

"Is he also your lover?" He shook his head. "No, don't answer that—it's none of my business. After all, what difference does it make?"

"He's not my lover," she said quickly. He was right; it couldn't make any difference. But she wanted him to know.

He released a heavy breath, then his lips curved in a rueful, shamefaced smile. "I told myself I was a fool, that I had no right to feel jealous—and besides, it's against the law to hit a cop."

She returned the smile. But there was nothing at all funny about their situation. "You wouldn't want to hit Blaine, anyway. He's too nice."

"Then why isn't he your lover?"

She shrugged and looked away toward the glowing logs in the fireplace. "I'm not attracted to him in that way."

"Does he want to marry you?"

"I think so. Blaine is definitely the marrying kind. And I'm sure he'll make someone a wonderful husband. He's caring, strong, decent..."

"But?" The urgency in his voice made her look at him again. His keen gaze bore into her. "Is he the kind of man who'd take away your freedom, Lucy?"

For a long moment she didn't answer. Then she finally said slowly, "No. I don't believe he would. He's strong and decisive, but he doesn't feel the need to dominate."

"So it must be something else, then. Not just the fear of losing your precious independence."

"I told you, I'm just not interested in him, in that way." She felt trapped and edgy. "And besides, who said anything about fear? I'm not afraid of anything. I just like being in control of my own life."

"But why do you feel you have to be alone in order to do that?"

"I don't." She shook her head vigorously. But she suddenly realized he was right. She did feel that way.

The blue eyes pinned her down. "You're not being absolutely honest, are you?"

"I guess not," she had to admit. "I do like Blaine, and it's not that I'm not attracted to him, but I don't want to get married. I don't want any part of that sort of relationship."

"Why not? What's wrong with marriage?"

"Marriage just means slavery." It was out before she realized what she'd said.

His brows rose a fraction. "That's a pretty harsh judgment. You've never been married before, I presume."

Looking down at her hands, clasped tightly in her lap, she gave voice to the thoughts she'd never expressed to anyone, not even Bea. "No, but I watched my mother being a slave to my father's every wish, regardless of my needs, or her own. All that mattered was keeping him happy."

She was shocked at the words that came tumbling out of her, the bitterness she'd never even suspected was there.

"You sound like you were jealous of your father."

"No! I loved him," she retorted vehemently.

"But you're angry at him," he said quietly.

For the first time, she realized that was absolutely true. She was angry with both of them—her father for being so selfish and needy, and her mother for choosing her father's needs over those of her child.

Her voice tightened as a lump rose in her throat. "She never wanted to go on that trip, or any of the trips. She was afraid of flying, especially in small planes."

Her clasped hands tightened, her fingers digging into each other painfully. "If only she'd spoken up for herself, she'd still be alive today."

"And you're angry with her because she didn't." His quiet voice cut through the sudden silence. "Because she died and left you."

"I'm angry with her for being so weak." The words emerged in a furious whisper. "Love made her weak."

"And you're afraid it'll make you weak, too. Is that why you've been avoiding it?"

Absolute silence fell, broken by a hissing log in the fire. Suddenly she looked up at him. "I haven't been avoiding it, I just haven't found it. I haven't met anyone who made me feel...whatever it is you're supposed to feel when you fall in love."

The way she felt around David? No. You had to know someone before you could love them.

"Maybe you just haven't given it a chance," David said quietly. "Love needs time to grow. It doesn't just come at you like a thunderbolt out of the blue."

A thunderbolt. Like the feeling that had hit her when she first saw him? But that wasn't love; it was just sex. And like any other thunderbolt, it might sizzle with a billion megawatts of electricity, but it dissipated into thin air a second later.

She turned her gaze back toward the glowing embers of the fire. "I agree with you about love needing to grow, but—"

"But you don't want it to," he interrupted.

She couldn't refute that—not with conviction.

"I know it's none of my business, but I think you need to talk about this, Lucy. Everyone needs love in their life. It's not healthy to deny it to yourself." Now he looked into the fire for a moment, a little self-consciously. "But I have to admit, I don't like to think about you with another man."

His words gave her a jolt. He was jealous? The thought filled her with a warm glow that she strove to quell. It couldn't be that.

"I know I have no right to feel this way," he added. "I shouldn't even be talking about it."

It was only because they couldn't act on these urges. It was the lure of forbidden fruit, making him feel this possessiveness.

"No. It only makes things worse," she said softly. "But you have no reason to be jealous. I've only had two serious relationships, and I didn't lose my heart in either of them. I thought it was because I don't have a heart to lose, but I suppose you might be right. I've been avoiding love."

"So why did you get into these relationships in the first place?"

He was posing questions she'd never asked herself before. "I guess I have the normal needs—sex, companionship. What I don't need is emotional dependency." For the first time, she'd put it into words. It was a bizarre awakening.

"So what was it about these men that made them

suitable?'' There was a slight edge to the seemingly casual question.

She didn't want to meet the look in his eyes. "Well, I met John when we were seniors at college. We dated for almost a year, but we both knew from the start that when school finished we'd go separate ways. Neither of us felt ready to settle down. And then there was Ethan. He was up here from Toronto on a two-year contract with the Ministry of Natural Resources."

His gaze searched her face. "Was that why you let yourself get involved with him, because you knew he'd be leaving?"

She slowly nodded her head. A pattern was beginning to emerge that she'd never suspected. "Boy, Freud would have a field day with my psyche, wouldn't he?''

"That's what's wrong with Blaine, isn't it? He's not going anywhere."

Just like a jigsaw puzzle, all the pieces were falling into place, and she hadn't even seen it until he'd pointed it out.

"You're right. That's exactly the problem," she admitted—to herself as much as to David. "I guess I've been avoiding any relationship where I'd run the risk of getting in too deep—gravitating toward men whose situations make it easy to call it quits. And I'm still doing it, aren't I? Because you're the most unsuitable of them all." *And the most dangerous*, she added silently.

She couldn't read his expression as the firelight danced in his blue eyes. "Now that you know what you've been doing, do you think your feelings for Blaine could change?"

"No," she said quietly. "Why should they? Maybe I

understand myself a little better now, but love is still a destructive emotion. If it exists at all. If I have the capacity to feel it. No, I prefer to be free, thank you.''

''Free to do what?''

She could only stare at him, her mind blank.

''You really don't know, do you?'' he said. ''You've spent a lot of time thinking about what you don't want, but what about what you *do* want?''

Now her mind felt as if it were turning inside out. ''Why do you have to ask me all these questions? Why do you have to bring this stuff up? I was perfectly happy with the way my life was going. Now suddenly you come along, out of the blue, and make me feel as if I don't know myself anymore, that I don't know where I'm going.''

''*Do* you know where you're going? What does your future look like to you? Do you plan to grow old in this house? Are you really free, or are you a prisoner, shackled by fear and distrust?'' he asked earnestly.

His questions raised too many frightening uncertainties. She felt angry and resentful. ''What do you know about all this stuff, anyway? You don't even remember your own name.''

He leaned forward, his expression intense. ''Don't let fear keep you from loving, Lucy. It doesn't have to mean giving up anything.''

She shook her head furiously. ''I disagree with you. And it's not just a question of giving something up. Look at Bea. She didn't willingly give up anything. She was robbed. Love robbed her of the part of herself that died with Wilfred Evans. No, I'm quite happy being emotionally independent.''

But was she? Right now she desperately needed David to hold her. An aching need filled her that couldn't be suppressed, and he must have read it on her face.

He was out of his chair and standing beside her in two strides. He pulled her up into his arms and held her close as she burrowed her head into his shoulder, pressing her cheek against the soft sweater.

"Poor Lucy, you're so confused right now. And I'm not helping the situation." He gently stroked her hair, soothing her.

It felt so good to be held, but very soon it wasn't enough. There was one thing she wasn't at all confused about; how much she wanted him to make love with her—right here, right now.

Some small part of her was shocked, but the rest of her didn't care. She needed him; she *wanted* him.

Blindly, she lifted her face, her lips meeting his unerringly, her mouth opening hungrily to his. He responded with warmth and tenderness, but she could feel his restraint.

It suddenly occurred to her that he understood her need for comfort, and he was giving it, but that he had no desire to go beyond this point. He wouldn't make love to her. And the last thing she needed right now was a rejection.

Breaking free, she gently pushed him away.

"I'm sorry." She stepped back and looked down at her hands, twisting them nervously together.

"What for?" He stood very still, his voice soft and husky in the quiet room.

She lifted her gaze to meet his again. "I started this whole mess by—"

"By opening the door?" His mouth curved in a rueful smile, but she didn't smile back.

"By not being stronger and more in control of myself." She took a deep breath and crossed her arms. "You could have a family waiting for you." Her voice tightened with guilt. "But I still want you...."

He sighed. Pacing over to the window, the curtains still open, he leaned one hand on the frame and stared out into the night. The light that spilled out of the room caught and sparkled on the nearest flakes of snow as they swirled and danced.

He turned his head to look at her again. "I try to imagine belonging to someone, and I can't. Even if I do, I find it difficult to feel anything for a woman I don't remember. Yes, I may very well have a wife and children, but right now they're just an abstract concept—they're not real to me. *You* are real. The way you make me feel is real."

A tremor of fear shook her. "The way you make me feel is real, too. But I know what makes you even more attractive is that you're a mystery man, a dream lover, with no ties that bind. It all makes perfect sense now."

Finally, she had it all figured out. So why didn't that put her mind at ease?

"IT'S STOPPED!" Lucy looked out the living-room window, hardly believing what she saw.

She'd just come down for a midafternoon cup of tea, and felt more encouraged than she had in days. Although the sky hung low and dark, only a few flakes drifted down and the wind had died completely.

All day long she'd hidden upstairs in her office, but the hours had dragged interminably and she'd gotten practically nothing done because David continued to intrude on her thoughts.

It was all very well to theorize that understanding

the attraction would make it easier to fight. Putting the theory into practice was something else completely. And knowing that the feelings were mutual made it almost impossible.

"Don't get your hopes up." Bea was busy watering the towering Ficus Benjamina that occupied one corner of the living room. "This is just a little lull. I heard the lunchtime weather forecast from Collingwood. It's going to get really bad tonight."

"Well, I'm going to get out in the fresh air while it lasts." She'd been cooped up too long and the breather would do her a world of good. "I won't be gone long." She turned and headed out of the room.

"Take David with you," Bea called after her. "He's looking a little peaked. I'm sure some fresh air would do him good, too."

She found him in the kitchen, peeling carrots. Bea was right. He did look pale.

"Do you cross-country ski?" she asked without preamble.

He shrugged. "I have no idea."

"Care to find out?"

"If you don't mind my tagging along."

Bea followed Lucy into the kitchen with the watering can in her hand. "Now don't go too far. The snow could start up again anytime. That western sky looks pretty threatening. And David shouldn't overdo it."

"Don't worry, we'll only go as far as the fence line."

In the mudroom she rummaged in the big built-in cupboard that held racks of skis and shelves of boots, until she found a pair that looked as if they might fit him, along with a pair of skis.

"Here, try these on for size." She handed him the

boots and propped the skis against the wall by the back door.

He sank down on the pine bench beside the cupboard and slid one foot into the boot. She stepped back into the closet and brought out her own boots, skis and poles.

He gave her an uncertain sideways glance. "Are you sure you want me along? You said you could only handle this as long as we kept apart."

She bent her head to slip on her own boots. "How much trouble can we get into outside, on skis?"

For a long moment he said nothing. Then he asked, "Why do you have all this extra equipment, anyway?"

She finished tying her laces and stood straight. "For our guests. Even in the winter, we're usually quite busy on the weekends. But in this kind of weather, everyone stays put."

The crisp, cold air hit her face as she stepped out the back door. She showed David how to snap the boots into and out of the ski bindings, then led the way across the field.

The skis sank only a little into the smooth unbroken snow, but Lucy could tell how deep it lay—almost even with the top of the split-rail fence.

They still had a few acres of land around the house, like this lovely open field filled with milkweed and butterflies in the summer, and bordered by hundred-year-old maples planted by the pioneering Westons.

At first she led the way across the pristine blanket of snow, and David followed in her tracks. But soon he was skiing at her side, with a smooth, powerful rhythm. He might not remember, but she would be willing to bet he'd skied many times before.

In only a few minutes, they had reached the fence

that bordered the highway. The road was barely discernible. Fresh snow had covered it again, obliterating the earlier work of the plows.

Looking across to the snow-covered pine wood on the other side of the road, she paused and leaned on her poles, breathing hard from the exertion but feeling exhilarated by the exercise.

This had to be the worst winter she could remember. They hardly ever closed down the highway because of snow, but it had been unusable for most of the past week.

David had skied a little farther along the fence and stood almost on top of it. She started to turn around. It was time they were getting back. This was quite enough for David's first time out, and she could feel the wind picking up again.

"Hey, wait!"

She turned back and saw he was leaning over, looking intently at something in the snow-filled ditch on the other side.

She skied over to join him. He glanced at her, then pointed downward.

"Look."

She followed the direction of his gloved finger to see something black protruding above the snow. At first she didn't know what it was. Then she realized it was the tread of a tire. It was awful, what people did to mess up the countryside.

Then she looked at his stunned face, and back to the tire, and suddenly realized what she was seeing.

When there was no snow, that ditch was three feet deep. She wasn't just seeing a tire; there was a vehicle under there.

9

DAVID DROPPED HIS POLES and leaned over to unsnap the ski bindings.

She stared at him, confused. "What are you doing?"

"I'm going to find out if that's my car."

"Are you crazy? If you take off those skis, you'll sink up to your armpits. Besides, it'll take hours to dig that out, and we probably don't have even a few minutes. Look at the sky."

He paused and glanced up at the low clouds the color of lead, then muttered a curse under his breath. For the first time, she saw impatience on his face.

"Why don't we go back to the house, call the police and tell them what we've found," she suggested reasonably. "As soon as the weather clears, they'll be able to have it dug out."

He shook his head and grabbed up his poles again. "No way. As soon as the weather clears, *I'll* dig it out. The police will have a lot more on their hands than my car."

"You're only assuming it's your car," she argued.

"It's a pretty safe bet."

She peered into the ditch. It would mean digging down through four feet of snow. "Nevertheless, it'll be a lot of work, and perhaps you shouldn't try—"

"If you think I can sit around and twiddle my thumbs while my identity could be only a few shovelfuls away, you're way off in your calculations." Pushing off on his skis, he started to head back toward the dark bulk of the house.

He set a swift pace, and she followed reluctantly. The soft swish of their skis was almost lost in the whine of the rising wind.

What was the matter with her? From the way she was behaving, one might think she *didn't want* him to find out who he was. But that was absurd!

A blast of Puccini hit them as they walked in the back door. Bea had Luciano Pavarotti on the stereo. They found her in the living room, doing her best to accompany him—at the top of her lungs, in an enthusiastic but quavery soprano—as she dusted the furniture.

Lucy caught his eye and somehow knew they were both wondering how Bea would take the news. But her great-aunt shrugged it off without a qualm.

"There's a car in that ditch every winter." Bea waved the feather duster across the china ornaments on the mantel. "It's the worst corner for accidents."

"But it could be David's car!"

"It could be, and then again, maybe not." She went back to her dusting, jauntily warbling away to *La Bohème.*

Typical Bea. Her motto was, why worry until you had something to worry about. If only *she* could be that sanguine.

Lucy looked at David, standing by the window, and shrugged. He smiled back, but she could see his preoccupation. He turned and gazed out into the thickening snow. Shoving his hands into his pockets, he leaned against the side of the deep window frame, with that lean and supple grace that sent a tremor of longing through her.

Hurrying out into the hall, she called the police station to report finding the car. Blaine answered. She told him of David's intention to dig out the car as soon as the snow stopped, and Blaine promised they would get a tow truck out there as soon as the road was open.

For the rest of the afternoon, she kept herself busy in the kitchen helping Bea with dinner, but her thoughts spun madly in a fever of impatience. Did that car really hold the secret to David's identity? Did she even want to know?

While dinner was in the oven, she and Bea got out the Double Wedding Ring quilt they were working on and sat sewing, while David prowled restlessly around the room. Clearly frustrated and chafing at the confinement, he went from window to window, watching the blizzard. The relentless wind made the huge, bare trees sway and bend like meadow grass.

He remained quiet and preoccupied. Every now and then, she would catch him watching her, his eyes dark, a frown creasing his brow. But she couldn't tell what was going through his mind.

After dinner, they went back to quilting, but by eight-thirty, Bea was yawning.

"I'm going to have an early night," she announced, folding up her side of the quilt and standing.

Coming out of his abstraction, David turned from the window. "You do look tired. Are you feeling all right?" He gave Bea a searching look, and Lucy noticed a trace of guilt in his eyes. "I'm sorry I've been so preoccupied today. I know I haven't been much help to you."

"Don't be silly. I've already told you your help isn't needed." She patted his shoulder as she passed by on her way out of the room. At the threshold, she stopped and turned. "I don't know why you're standing around stewing like this. The wind has died, and it's barely snowing at all right now. Go out there, dig out that infernal car and find out if it belongs to you."

"But it's too late!" Lucy insisted, feeling panicky all of a sudden. "Tomorrow would be much better. It might not be a good idea for David to overexert himself. It's been a long day."

"And it'll be a long night if he just lies there worrying about it."

"You're absolutely right. Why wait until the morning?" David moved away from the window and followed Bea out into the hall.

"Good. That's settled, then. Good night, kids."

As Bea went up the stairs, Lucy followed David into the mudroom. She reached out and grabbed his arm to stop him. "You're not going to take her seriously and go out there?"

"Why not?" He looked out the window beside the door. "The snow has stopped completely. There's even a moon coming through."

"But it's so late." Even to her own ears, the excuse sounded feeble.

His blue eyes were searching. "What's the matter, Lucy? Don't you want to know who I am?"

"I did. I *do*, but..." How could she tell him something so unforgivable? But she couldn't evade his probing gaze, and finally blurted out her fear. "Once you find out who you are and where you belong, you'll be on your way."

There. She'd said it.

He didn't say anything for a long moment, and the silence gathered around them in the shadowy room. He just looked at her, and she saw his eyes darken. "But that's what you wanted."

"And I still do, but not so soon." She realized just then that all they had was this moment. Whatever he learned from that car would be irrevocable.

Her breath came faster. "Hold me, hold me now," she said, her voice a mere whisper. "You may not be able to later."

She saw it in his eyes: He knew it, too.

Suddenly a soft, tormented groan came from his throat, and he pulled her to him. His arms wrapped around her, crushing her to his hard chest. His lips covered hers; his tongue invaded her mouth in a desperate kiss.

A wild torrent of pleasure flooded her senses. Weak with longing, she responded even more urgently. She might never have the chance to experience anything like this again. She wanted to extract every ounce of pleasure from this wonderful moment.

He caressed her feverishly, his hands sliding over her back, over the curve of her hips. With another frustrated groan, he began to pull up her sweatshirt, and the T-shirt underneath, until he was touching the bare skin of her back. Her knees weakened as his other hand slid down to caress her bottom and pull her hips against his.

She could feel how much he wanted her, and she clung to his shoulders to support herself as liquid heat pooled between her thighs. She pressed herself closer, and he responded by grinding against her as the kiss deepened. That exquisite pressure began building inside her. If she could just move against him a little closer... Another moment and she would be there....

Then his hands captured her hips and held her still. He pulled away, and she could see the effort it took.

His chest was heaving, and a dull red flush edged his cheekbones. His desperate gaze roamed over her face. "Lucy... That's as far as we can let this go. Or we'll do something we'll both regret."

He was right. She knew he was right.

"Okay." She nodded, struggling for breath, trying to keep her legs from shaking. "But I'm coming with you. You'll need my help."

"I was hoping you'd say that." He smiled. It was obvious he was trying to defuse the sexual tension that had come so close to exploding. Thank God he hadn't lost *his* reason.

SAILING IN A DRAMATIC sky of slow-moving clouds, the full moon poured down its cold light, making the snow gleam like a field of diamonds, and throwing everything into high relief.

The wind had died to nothing, and although the air was crisp and chilly, the cold didn't seem to penetrate as they skied across the open field in the dead silence of the winter night.

When they reached the car, David unstrapped the shovels that he'd carried on his back.

Suddenly Lucy heard the whine of a snowmobile approaching along the road, and the beam of a headlight came around the bend. The next moment it was pulling up beside them. When the rider removed his helmet, she saw it was Blaine.

"Had a feeling you'd be out here. Thought you could use an extra set of hands."

He was looking at David, and she suddenly realized that they hadn't met. She hurriedly made the introductions and the two men shook hands—a surrealistic picture in the moonlight.

Blaine reached into the storage compartment of the snowmobile and took out a fold-up shovel. "As you can see, I came prepared."

David smiled. "Thanks. I appreciate your help."

They got to work digging down where David imagined the front door to be. She had no idea how long they worked, sunk to their waists in snow, but soon her brow was wet with sweat, and she got so warm that she took off her heavy ski sweater.

Eventually they could see the bottom of the door, battered and scratched, and then the handle came into sight. At last they'd cleared the whole side and a smashed-in window was exposed.

Quickly dropping his shovel, David got down on his stomach. He pulled out a flashlight from his pocket, and shone it inside.

"The snow didn't really blow in," his muffled voice reported. "It's quite dry in here. There's a jacket and— Ah."

"Have you found something?" she asked anxiously. At least her worst fear had been allayed. There was no dead body in there. Thank God.

David wriggled backward and finally emerged. Sinking back on his knees, he shone the flashlight on the small rectangular item in his hand. She looked over his shoulder. It was a plastic folder containing a driver's license.

Even though his hair was slightly longer now, there was no doubt that the face in the photo was his. When she saw the name on the license, she caught her breath with a little gasp.

"David Quinn." He said the name slowly, as if trying it out on his tongue.

"If you give me your license, I'll run it through the computer and we'll get some information for you."

Lucy looked up with a start. For a moment, she'd forgotten Blaine was there at all.

David handed the license to him, then bent down again to pull out the jacket. She watched him digging through the pockets until he drew out a wallet. She held the flashlight as he rifled through it, pulling out credit cards and a few business cards with only the name, a Toronto address, and a phone number. There was also some money—five twenties.

"No photos." Her breath clouded the cold air. There was nothing personal, no other hint of who this man might be, or who might be important to him.

He gave her a steadfast, serious look. With a sinking heart, she realized they still knew virtually nothing about his life. He could still be married, or living with someone.

"I have to phone this number." David looked grim.

"Now? It must be very late." Cold dread trickled through her. "Why don't you wait till morning?" It would only be putting off the inevitable, but at least she would have one more night.

"No, now." His eyes were dark and somber in the pale light. "I can't wait that long."

"If nothing else, it'll put your mind at ease, in case there's someone at home worrying about you," Blaine said, with the calm good sense she usually found reassuring. He stowed away the shovel in the snowmobile again, and zipped up his heavy jacket. "Don't worry about the car. We'll take care of it."

She turned to Blaine. "I don't know how to thank you for coming along and helping like this."

"I wouldn't say no to a hot drink." He picked up his helmet, and paused before slipping it on.

"Of course. You must come back to the house." She felt ashamed of the impulse that just wanted Blaine to go away so she could be alone with David. "You'll be there before us. Why don't you put the kettle on?"

"I've got a better idea. Hop on the back and I'll give you two a ride."

David slipped the wallet into his pocket and went to retrieve the jacket. An eerie feeling crept over her. It was almost identical to the navy parka he had bought in town.

Wedged between Blaine and David, she rode back to the house on the snowmobile, clutching her skis tightly. It was too bizarre—riding through the moonlit, snowy landscape with the two men in her so-called life.

If she had to choose, the smart choice would be the man in front. The trouble was, she wanted the one in the back.

Had it already happened to her? That loss of her precious freedom, despite how carefully she'd guarded it?

She was so confused. Maybe it was a good thing Blaine was coming back with them. David had been right when he'd said they couldn't give in to their desires. It would only complicate things even more.

When they got back to the house, Lucy went straight

in and put on the kettle. Blaine followed her, pulled out a chair at the big kitchen table, and sat down.

David took his time getting his coat and boots off. Through the open doorway, he watched the other two.

So, this was Blaine. David felt bleak inside. The guy was everything Lucy could want. Big, blond and handsome, he was also obviously a really decent man, coming out to help as he had. And just as obviously, he was crazy about Lucy. He sat watching her with quiet devotion as she went about making the tea, her movements swift and graceful.

If *he* cared about her, he should be glad she had someone like Blaine around. But it made him feel like hell. And he had no right to feel that way.

He went through into the hall to make the phone call. It didn't matter whether he was living with someone or not; he still had no right to involve himself in Lucy's life. He had no right to involve himself in anybody's life until he got his own sorted out—if he ever did; after all, there was no guarantee his memory would ever return.

He picked up the receiver. The old rotary phone clicked away interminably as he dialled the long-distance number. A strange, numb detachment settled over him when he heard it begin to ring.

It rang twice, and then he heard the click of it being picked up. Acute resentment gripped him for a moment. But then that dead detachment came over him again. Whatever would be, would be.

His own voice came over the line. "David Quinn, here. I can't take your call right now, but leave a message at the sound of the beep."

He put down the phone as the numbness vanished in a surge of joy.

He walked quickly back into the kitchen. Lucy and Blaine looked up from where they sat at the table. He could see the tense expectation on Lucy's face as she got to her feet. Blaine had gotten up, too, and stood close behind her in a protective way.

David tried to keep the excitement out of his voice. "I got my answering machine. It sounds like I live alone."

A slow, disbelieving excitement began to blaze in Lucy's eyes, and it brought him to his senses. He looked away. He still wasn't free to involve himself with Lucy, whether he had a wife or not.

"Well, I'll be going home now and let you guys get some rest," Blaine announced, breaking the silence. He moved forward and held out a hand to David. "I'll call you in the morning and tell you anything I've been able to find out."

David took his hand and shook it. "Thanks for your help." He was able to meet the other man's eyes quite calmly. The earlier antagonism he'd felt toward Blaine had dissipated. Blaine had a right to pursue Lucy. He didn't. And he wouldn't.

While she saw Blaine out, he went straight up to his room. He had to remove himself from temptation.

But only a minute later, his door opened. Lucy came in, shut it quietly behind her and leaned against it. Her green eyes glowed in the light of the small, shaded lamp by the bed. He could feel her seductive power drawing him in against his will.

"I don't think this is a good idea, Lucy. I think you should go back to your room."

"Why? Don't you want me, too?"

"It's got nothing to do with what I want. I'm trying desperately to do the right thing. Don't make it so difficult for me."

"The right thing? What is the right thing?"

"I don't want to screw up your life."

"People's lives don't get screwed up by one-night stands. We both know that's all this could be. You have to understand what happened to me that night, the night you fell at my feet. Something passionate inside me burst free—something I never even knew was there. I want to explore that part of me. Please, don't send me away."

Suddenly his eyes glittered with a hot intensity that made her heart begin to race. He crossed the floor in two strides and stopped mere inches from her. The heat from his body, the scent of his skin, drugged her, assaulted her senses beyond enduring.

He stood looking down at her. "I've wanted you from the moment I opened my eyes and saw you lying there beside me," he murmured, his husky voice edged with urgency.

He took her into his arms, and she melted, blindly seeking his lips. His mouth closed hungrily over hers—a hunger that matched her own.

Finally he pulled away breathlessly and looked down into her face, his eyes gleaming with desire. "Last chance. We should stop now."

"I don't think I could if I tried," she whispered.

He swung her up into his arms.

"David, be careful, your head..."

His mouth closed over hers, stifling her protest with an urgent kiss, then he pulled away. "It's not my head that hurts right now." He gave a breathless chuckle that turned to a groan. "If I don't make love to you this minute, I'll die."

With her arms tightly wound around his neck, she gave him a shaky, provocative smile. "Can you wait long enough to get to the bed?"

"That would be about the extent of my patience." His strained voice told her that his control was fast slipping away. With long strides, he carried her over to the four-poster and laid her down.

Excitement filled her—a bubbling swirling fever of anticipation like nothing she'd ever experienced.

Silence closed around them as he leaned over her, looking down at her in the soft light from the Tiffany bedside lamp. A faint flush tinged his cheekbones. Lucy could barely catch her breath, and her pounding heart seemed about to leap out of her chest. Could this actually be real, or was she dreaming?

Slowly, he reached out a hand and cupped her face, and she felt the delicious abrasion of his thumb caressing the fullness of her lips, coaxing them to part. Her tongue darted out, then languorously swept across the tip of his thumb.

His eyes clouded with desire, darkening to cobalt. Her lids fluttered closed at the exquisite sensations racing through her. Tiny shivers trembled over every inch of her body as his hand slowly traveled down over her throat. Slowly, ever so slowly, his fingers slid beneath the neck of her sweater and lightly stroked the spot where her pulse vibrated in a frantic rhythm.

She opened her eyes to see his gaze locked on hers as he watched her response, catching every nuance, his hunger burning hot and pure.

His trembling hand slid down to curve around her breast, swollen and aching for him beneath the sweater and T-shirt. Even through the layers of clothing, she felt a jolt of molten heat between her thighs when his thumb stroked over her taut nipple.

A groan tore from her. He came down beside her, pulled her into his arms and covered her mouth with his. He kissed her slowly and urgently, silencing her, then pulled away for a moment.

"Shh... We don't want to wake Bea," he whispered shakily against her lips.

"That's for sure," Lucy agreed in a fervent murmur, as she began to tug at his belt buckle.

His mouth covered hers again, more urgently than before, feeding on her lips as their tongues hungrily entwined. She hardly noticed that he'd already disposed of her belt and had her jeans unzipped.

He pulled away from her and quickly helped her off with her sweater and T-shirt while she did the same for him. The sound of labored breathing filled the room as they undressed each other completely, with whispered murmurs and soft moans of pleasure punctuating the removal of each garment.

Finally they lay down again, facing each other, close, but not touching. His gaze roamed over her. Reverently, he reached up and cupped one heavy, swollen breast with his long, sensitive fingers.

"You're so beautiful. Your body is so exquisite, so perfect," he said shakily.

"You, too," she whispered, sliding her hands over his chest. Her touch lingered on the smooth, rough circle of scar tissue on his shoulder.

He flinched a little, and looked down at the old wound with a grimace. "Not so perfect, after all."

For a moment, she felt a stab of worry. A bullet wound. But no. Everything she knew about him contradicted the idea that he could have done something bad.

She leaned forward and pressed her lips to the warm, smooth patch of flesh, then looked up into his eyes. "You're wrong—you're quite beautiful."

To her amazement, she saw a red flush graze his cheekbones. She smiled and trailed her hands down his flat stomach, tracing the same path with her gaze.

Her fingertips touched him, and he flinched, as if in pain. He closed his eyes with a groan as she took him completely into her hand. His silky length felt hot and hard—even harder as she began to stroke him back and forth.

"Lucy, please..." he said, his voice ragged. Then he reached out and pulled her to him, ravaging her lips while his hand moved down to cup her bottom and press her hips tight against him, trapping her hand. He drew away with a gasp. "Give me a break—"

"David, there's something I've wanted to do ever since I first saw you. Something I've never done before..."

He groaned. "What are you trying to do? Torture me?"

"Not tonight," she said with a grin, and gently pushed him over, then straddled him. He lay stretched out on his back, the soft light gilding the firm, carved length of his body. She caught her breath.

"I want to touch you all over," she said in a husky whisper.

With her hands she explored him, letting her palms slide over the smooth skin of his chest, bending to encircle one brown nipple with her lips.

He let out a groan of agony. "Okay, but don't blame me if I start without you."

She giggled. "I'll just make you do it again."

Delicately, she caressed the hard little nub with her tongue. She heard his sharp indrawn breath, but he didn't pull away. He threaded his hands through her hair, massaging her head, and shifted beneath her so that one thigh pressed between hers, where she wanted to feel him so badly. But not yet. Her hands slid down over his flat stomach, his flesh quivering at her touch.

"Are you sure you've never done this before?" He gasped.

"No, never," she murmured against him as her lips traced the same path. And then her fingers closed around the hot, hard length of him and a moment later her mouth followed.

"Lucy..." Her name became a sigh on his lips.

Arousal tore through her, sensations unlike any she'd ever experienced before. She'd never wanted to do this with any other man, and the wanton urgency of this feeling was slightly shocking—shocking, but an incredible turn-on.

Suddenly, he gripped her arms and hauled her on top of him. He took her mouth, kissing her breathless before releasing her.

She shivered uncontrollably. He was hot and hard against her. "I want to feel you inside me more than I've ever wanted—" She never finished the sentence.

With a sharp indrawn breath, he lifted his hips and

slid into her, burying himself. But for a long moment he didn't move, just stared up at her, an unfathomable expression in his blue eyes.

"What's the matter?" She could barely speak.

"Nothing." The word emerged on a gasp. "You're so tight. You feel so good. I wish I could describe the sensation. I'm afraid if I move, it'll all be over. But I can't wait any longer."

Suddenly his control snapped. He rolled her onto her back and drove deeply into her—slowly, at first, and then faster, harder. She wrapped her legs around his straining buttocks and matched him, thrust for thrust.

He gave a cry he smothered against her mouth as she felt his pulsing release. At the same moment, her own orgasm exploded with a power that took her very breath away.

The racking shudders went on and on as their arms tightened around each other. Finally, the spasms ebbed, leaving her spent and clinging to him. With one last convulsive movement, David, too, went still and collapsed onto her.

This was so much more than just the most overwhelming physical experience she'd ever had. But she was too exhausted to even wonder about the enormity of the emotion holding her in thrall.

After a few minutes, he rolled onto his side, pulling her into his arms, and before she knew it, blissful sleep washed over her....

AT THE SOUND OF QUICK footsteps, Lucy woke with a start. It was Bea, heading downstairs. Soft gray light filled the room. It was morning already.

She lifted her head to look at him and felt a quiver of pure joy at the sight of his face, so beautiful and defenseless in sleep.

A fleeting twinge of guilt assailed her—she shouldn't have stayed here all night—but it vanished in an instant as she bent to lightly kiss his lips. Waking up beside him was heavenly.

She turned her head to glance out the window. Through the filmy lace she could see big, fat flakes of snow wafting down. It had started again. But now the thought of being trapped together no longer filled her with fear. Keen, sweet excitement tingled through her. Right now, she didn't want to be anywhere except with David.

With a reluctant sigh, she began carefully slipping out of bed. She didn't want Bea to find out she'd spent the night with him.

A hand slid down her back and over her bottom, gently caressing her bare skin. She turned to see his eyes were open now, and his mouth curved in a warm, provocative smile.

"Bea is up already. She's just gone downstairs," she said halfheartedly.

"She won't come in here," he murmured, laying her gently down again. He kissed a tender path over her body to the dark curls between her thighs.

She couldn't help sighing in pleasure. "She might." She struggled to focus on speech as liquid heat swirled and gathered low in her belly.

"Besides, it's my turn to repay the favor," he said, his voice muffled as his tongue probed and found the spot that had every nerve end in her body quivering with fire.

With a shaky sigh, she let her head fall back and gave herself up to the pleasure.

An hour later, she somehow managed to part from him long enough to get showered and dressed. They were reunited on the landing, where she returned his warm smile and fell into his arms for a long, languorous kiss before they went downstairs for breakfast.

Before they reached the bottom of the stairs, she stopped him with a hand on his arm. "David," she said uncertainly. "I don't want Bea to know about this. We both know it's only temporary, but she'll jump to conclusions and end up disappointed."

"I understand. I wouldn't hurt Bea for the world." Quickly, he brushed his mouth against her lips before letting her go and assuming a bland expression.

Bea looked closely at them as they came into the kitchen. "Well, don't you two look like the cat that got the cream!"

Lucy felt her cheeks catch fire. "We've got some news."

Bea's blue, keen little eyes darted from one to the other. "News?"

"That car in the ditch belongs to me," David said gently. "We found my license and there's no doubt about it."

She looked up at him for a moment. "And your name?"

"David Quinn."

There was a small, triumphant glimmer in her smile. "So your name really is David, hmm? My, my... Coincidence or magic?"

Her eyes twinkled mischievously as she looked from

one to the other. Then the phone in the hall rang and she went to get it.

"It's for you, David." Bea's voice held an odd note as it filtered through from the hallway. "It's a woman called Cheryl Gallagher. She says…that she's your fiancée."

10

THE SILENCE ROARED in her ears. All the blood seemed to drain from her body and ice flooded her veins.

She looked at David. His face had gone deathly pale. He stood as if turned to stone.

If she had any doubts about the nature of her feelings for him, they had just been erased. She felt an aching, overwhelming sense of loss—as if part of herself had been wrenched away.

But from this moment on, she had to put those feelings aside—for his sake. And only for his sake could she do it.

"Come on, Bea. Let's go upstairs and give David some privacy." To her amazement, her voice emerged quite steady, betraying none of the confusion and pain tearing her apart inside.

"But David may need our support! This is going to be very difficult for him. After all, this Cheryl person is—"

"His fiancée," Lucy ruthlessly reminded her, at the same time bracing herself against the shaft of pain that tore through her.

David gave her a long, grave look, his eyes filled with self-condemnation. She knew he was blaming himself for the mess they were in, and she couldn't bear it. Or allow him to do it.

Somehow she managed a small, reassuring smile.

She knew what he had to do, and she was going to make it as easy for him as she could.

"I think he'd prefer his privacy." Taking her great-aunt's hand, she drew her quickly out of the room. Bea strained at her grip as they ascended the stairs.

"Privacy, shmivacy!" Bea finally pulled her to a halt at the top landing and glared at her indignantly. "Answer me this, missy. Where was his fiancée when he was lying practically at death's door?"

"At home in Toronto, worrying," Lucy said tightly, giving her great-aunt's hand another tug. "Come on, let's go up to my studio."

Bea yanked away her hand and perched it on her hip. "Why did it take her so long to notice he was missing?"

"I'm sure there's a very good explanation, but it's none of our business," she said firmly and turned away from her great-aunt's accusatory glare. If only she could believe that.

Lucy took the steep attic stairs two at a time, needing to get as far away as possible from the sound of his voice. She couldn't bear to hear it.

She flung open the door at the top of the stairs and stepped into the studio.

"But why should she be calling here now?" Bea's voice behind her brought her out of her abstraction. She turned to see her great-aunt standing in the doorway, her finely penciled eyebrows twin arcs of indignation. "She had her turn, and she obviously blew it. He was taken from her and sent to you...."

The worst part was that Lucy agreed with that. She actually felt angry and resentful toward this woman instead of guilty. She took a deep breath. Was she crazy?

"I guess the powers-that-be have changed their collective mind," Lucy said lightly, as waves of misery churned inside her. "He's got to go back. You're not going to argue with 'the all-knowing one,' are you?"

Bea opened her mouth, and then clamped her lips together, frustration and annoyance written all over her face.

Once again, she'd rendered her great-aunt speechless, but she was too heartsick to enjoy the moment.

As THE VOICES ABOVE died away, David stared at the old black phone sitting on the hall table and his frown deepened. Jamming his hands into the pockets of his jeans, he walked slowly toward it.

All he had to do was pick up that receiver, and he would be reconnected to his life. So why was he stalling? And why was his thinking less concerned about how this Cheryl must be feeling than about the shocking ease with which Lucy seemed ready to give him up?

But what did he expect? She'd said it herself; all she'd wanted was to explore the passion that had sprung up between them. She had called it a one-night stand. That was all it was to her.

But even if it weren't, she had integrity, which was far more than he could say about himself. He just wanted to stay here, hidden in the safe world Lucy and Bea had created for him. Was he a coward, or just confused?

Probably a little bit of both.

He picked up the phone, his jaw clenched so hard it

hurt. But the pain was no more than he deserved. He knew one thing for sure: He'd been a weak, irresponsible fool.

"David, here," he said tersely.

He heard a sharply indrawn breath. "David, is that you?" The soft and very feminine voice didn't spark any recognition at all, but it made his chest suddenly feel hollow. He couldn't breathe.

He clutched the receiver with cold, clammy hands. "Cheryl?" he began uncertainly, his mouth as dry as dust.

A shaky sigh of relief came over the line. "Thank God you're okay. When I called the lodge and they said you'd never arrived— Oh, David, you'll never know the terror I felt.... Even now, thinking about it..."

Lodge? What lodge? This all felt so unreal. Nothing clicked; nothing seemed familiar. He felt a numb detachment spreading through him.

"It's all right, Cheryl. I'm all right." The reassurance was just an automatic response, he realized.

"Where are you?" The anxiety in her voice didn't touch him in any personal way at all.

"I'm in Hazeldene. It's a little place up near Collingwood. I'm sorry you've been so worried. I would have called right away but—"

She broke in anxiously. "It's all right David, I understand. The police said you'd been in an accident, that you're suffering from amnesia."

"Yes, that's right."

"So you don't remember anything?" There was an odd, hesitant note in her voice.

"Nothing. I'm afraid to say that I...I don't even remember you." It sounded so cold—cruel, even. Yet it was the truth.

There was silence from the other end.

"But the doctor says it's only temporary," he continued.

But what if it wasn't? What if he was left with nothing but this void?

Lucy's face swam before him. Those glowing green eyes and soft, full lips. He smothered a groan, remembering how those lips had felt against his mouth, the way they'd looked after he'd kissed her, the way she'd tasted....

"I'm going to come up and get you, bring you home where you belong." Cheryl's voice sliced through his daydream.

With a shock, he realized that he wanted Lucy; wanted her right now, even while he talked to another woman who had a far greater claim on him. What kind of depraved monster did that make him?

"The roads up here are closed because of the storm." He gritted his teeth and tried to concentrate on the conversation. The overwhelming need for Lucy gripped him like a physical pain he had to fight to quell.

"As soon as the roads are clear, then," she said.

"It might take days." He couldn't help the surge of relief at that possibility. He shouldn't feel that way, but he did.

"Darling, I miss you so much, and I love you." Her voice became soft and intimate.

What was he supposed to say? He couldn't tell her he loved her. This woman was a stranger. He didn't feel anything for her.

Oh, yes, he did. He must. But he just didn't remember. The fact remained, however, that he'd pledged himself to marry her.

"I...I'm looking forward to seeing you again, Cheryl," he said finally, aware of how inadequate and awkward the words must sound.

"I'm going to pray the weather clears soon so I can come to you," she said fervently. "And then I'll never let you out of my sight again."

A cold, sick feeling came over him, and he felt an invisible net closing around him. He couldn't do this anymore, couldn't carry on this conversation. "I've got to go now, Cheryl."

"I'll call you when I'm on my way."

He said goodbye and quickly hung up. Then he lunged for the stairs, racing up them two at a time. On the landing, he saw Bea just emerging from her room, and knew she'd been waiting for him.

"Where's Lucy?" he asked desperately.

Bea turned her gaze to the ceiling.

"I've got to talk to her."

She patted his shoulder as she moved past him. "I'll be downstairs if anyone needs me."

Thank God she hadn't asked him any questions. Giving Bea's thin arm a squeeze of gratitude as she went by, he quickly climbed the stairs to the attic. At the open door, he paused.

Lucy had her back to him. Leaning her head against the top of the window frame, she stood looking out into the storm.

"Lucy..." he began, then stopped. What could he say? What did he want to say? "Lucy, I'm sorry for putting you in this terrible position."

"There's nothing to be sorry about." She didn't turn around.

"Yes, there is. I should never have given in to my...impulses. I knew all along, under the circumstances, I shouldn't have let things go so far. I should have controlled myself."

When she said nothing, he continued. "But I was weak and I did the one thing I promised myself I would never do. I've hurt you, and I can't forgive myself for that. But I am sorry."

"Don't, David." She could hear the pain in his voice, and turned to face him. He stood in the attic doorway; the misery in his eyes stabbed her in the heart.

She tried to keep her voice calm and even. "If anyone's responsible, we both know it's me. It was a one-night stand—nothing to get your knickers in a twist over, as Bea would say." She gave him a wry smile.

He didn't smile back—just held her gaze, his expression dark and brooding.

"Look, David, you opened my eyes, and my world. And I used you to experiment, to explore my...sexual potential. I should never have led you into doing something you now feel guilty about."

Shaking her head, she crossed her arms and rubbed herself. Despite her heavy sweater, she felt so cold. "I'm sorry, David. It was an experiment that got out of hand. But now it's time for you to go home."

"Yes, home," he said heavily.

She understood the fear and uncertainty that filled him right now. She'd felt that kind of helplessness before: the day she'd left her home in Toronto to come and live with Bea and Georgie.

"Just being at home again will stimulate your memory. You'll have your life back in no time."

"I'm sure you're right." He nodded, his blue eyes grim as they held hers. "I'll never forget you."

A wave of anguish swept through her, but she willed herself not to let it show. "I'll never forget you, either."

His expression hardened. "Will you be all right?"

Somehow she managed a cocky smile. Somehow she kept her voice strong and even. "Don't worry about me. I'll be fine."

He must never guess the truth—that she couldn't imagine being satisfied with her life again. Now she knew what she'd been missing. But this just proved she'd been right all along; getting emotionally involved only brought pain and disillusion.

"She's coming to get me when the roads open," he said, sounding distracted.

"She must be very anxious."

"Yes." He nodded, then a frown creased his brow. "Will you let me know from time to time how you're doing?"

Taking a deep breath, she swallowed the enormous lump that had formed in her throat. It was just guilt and his deep sense of responsibility that made him feel miserable—nothing more than that.

Except perhaps the understandable fear of leaving behind all that was safe and familiar and stepping into the unknown.

"I don't think that would be a very good idea for either of us."

He closed his eyes for a second, as if in acquiescence, then heaved a deep sigh and nodded slowly.

"I guess we'd better go downstairs and tell Bea." There was no point in putting off the inevitable. A few more painful hours, and he would be gone.

They went down to the kitchen and broke the news. Strangely enough, Bea reacted quite calmly.

"Well, this is unfortunate." A frown puckered her brow. "I can see you'll have to go back and straighten out your affairs. But you'll be back, young man. Don't you worry."

She patted his arm reassuringly, then walked into the pantry, leaving the two of them alone in the kitchen.

Lucy sighed. "There's no point in arguing, or trying to make her see reason. Eventually it's going to become obvious that you're not coming back, and then she'll have to accept it."

David nodded in agreement, but looked so grim that she couldn't stand seeing his pain another moment. How she yearned to comfort him, and to seek comfort for herself in his arms. But she had to ignore the almost-overpowering urge. Touching him would be suicidal.

The rest of that day dragged on. They were the most painful hours she'd endured since the day she'd received the news of her parents' death. All she wanted was to be close to him, and that was impossible.

That night the snow stopped. By eight the next morning the heavy rumble of the plows could be heard from the highway. At ten, the phone rang.

Bea called to David from the hall. Lucy sat at the kitchen table, hunched over a cup of coffee, trying not to hear.

He sounded subdued as he quietly said hello. A moment later, he appeared in the kitchen doorway, looking awkward. "I need directions how to get here."

Numbly, Lucy briefly outlined the quickest route from the city. He relayed the instructions, then said goodbye and came back to stand in the doorway again.

She could hardly bring herself to look at him, for fear he would see the depth of pain in her eyes.

"She said she'll be here by midafternoon. If she doesn't get lost, that is."

Lucy had the swift, fervent desire that she would do exactly that, then felt ashamed. Besides, that would only be delaying the parting.

"I guess I'd better go upstairs and pack my stuff," he said gruffly, then turned and left the kitchen.

JUST AFTER LUNCH, a knock sounded at the front door. Lucy put down the cards in her hand and looked across the coffee table at David. For the past hour they had been playing gin rummy with dogged persistence, although she knew very well that neither one of them was concentrating on the game.

"I'll get that," she said calmly, but her stomach gave a sickening lurch as she got to her feet.

Taking a deep breath to muster her courage, she went reluctantly to answer the door. A beautiful blonde in a long red coat stood on the porch, clutching her collar against the cold. Eagerness and anxiety were written all over her face.

Lucy's heart filled her chest like a lead weight. This was Cheryl? She was lovely—flawless, even. The anxiety on her face spoke loud and clear; this woman loved David.

"Are you Ms. Weston? I'm Cheryl Gallagher, David's fiancée."

"Please, come in," she said belatedly, suddenly realizing that she'd just been staring at the woman while the cold wind swirled in through the open doorway.

But Cheryl was looking past her, and her angelically pale face lit up with a tremulous smile. Lucy turned to see David standing in the hall behind her. Cheryl flew past and launched herself into his embrace, hugging him tightly.

Looking slightly dazed, he closed his arms uncertainly around the woman who clung to him. Lucy turned away and almost ran into the kitchen.

Stopping in the middle of the room, she leaned on the pine table and took a deep breath. It hurt so much, seeing them in each other's arms. Would the twisting pain deep inside ever go away?

She had to pull herself together, but she couldn't deny that she wished she knew a spell that would make Cheryl vanish from the face of the earth.

But no matter how fervently she wanted things to be different, he had to leave. And she had to get on with her life.

First things first, though. She had to tell Bea that David's fiancée was here. If only Lucy dared leave her in ignorance until after they were gone. She wasn't looking forward to this meeting.

Bea was in the pantry, sorting through bunches of dried herbs laid out on the counter.

Lucy paused in the doorway, her brow creased in a worried frown as she watched her for a moment. Then she softly cleared her throat, and her great-aunt looked up and gave her a loving smile.

"Bea, we have a visitor. It's David's fiancée, Cheryl."

The smile vanished. For a moment Bea stared as if she weren't even seeing her. Then suddenly she was all bustle and determination. Setting down the bundle of herbs in her hand, she smoothed her neatly coiled braid and hurried past into the kitchen.

"Come along, Lucy, I'm anxious to meet this young lady."

Lucy smothered a groan. Those brisk words meant trouble.

She followed her great-aunt through into the living room. Right now she couldn't bring herself to worry about what Bea might say or do. She had worries of her own. Cheryl would have to defend herself.

The red coat lay flung over the end of the couch where Cheryl sat in tailored black pants and an expensive-looking, gold-embroidered black sweater.

David sat in the armchair next to her, and she was showing him a photograph. More pictures spilled out of a thick envelope on her lap.

"And this was last summer, in the Bahamas. Remember that cute little cottage right on the beach?"

David had a picture in his hand and was looking blankly at the one she held out. Obviously nothing had clicked yet.

Lucy's heart went out to him. He looked shell-shocked.

"So, you're Cheryl! Don't get up."

As the woman glanced up, startled, Bea tottered over to the couch and plunked herself down beside her. Blatantly, she looked over the interloper from head to foot.

"Yes, yes, I am," Cheryl stammered, clearly a little taken aback.

"I'm Beatrice Weston. You must already have met my niece, Lucy."

The wide blue eyes darted over to Lucy as she stood awkwardly near the doorway. "Yes, I have... I mean...nice to meet you."

"Yes, very well," Bea said tersely. "So, you've come to take our David away, have you?"

"Yes... Thank you so much for taking such good care of him." Cheryl was clearly feeling ill at ease, and Lucy could hardly blame her. Bea had her small gimlet eyes pinned on the woman as if she were a specimen under a microscope.

"No thanks are necessary, young lady. We've come to care very much for David. But of course, you do too, right?" She tipped her head to one side and gave Cheryl a shrewd, penetrating look.

"Of course I do!" Cheryl's face went a little red, but she didn't hold Bea's glance. She turned to David and her smile seemed stiff. "Are you ready to go?"

"You must have been frantic when he went missing," Bea continued, as if Cheryl hadn't even spoken.

Definitely stiff now, she turned back to Bea. "I was worried sick, and imagining the worst."

"And yet it took you several days to file a report. Lucy and I both agreed that if David belonged to us, he'd be missed right away."

An oddly defensive look, compounded with a hint of fear, came into Cheryl's blue eyes. "He'd gone skiing. When he didn't come back I began to worry...."

"David, I'm surprised at you." Bea gave him a coquettish little smile. "I thought you would be the type

who would call the woman you loved to let her know
you'd arrived safely, or say good-night with some tan-
talizing phone sex...."

Everyone gasped.

"Bea!" Lucy protested, then closed her mouth. What
was the point of telling Bea to stop being outrageous?
She was obviously doing it on purpose, even though—
and it pained her to admit it—there was nothing *not* to
like about Cheryl.

The woman was beautiful, with a warm and ready
smile. Her love and concern for David were painfully
obvious. What was there not to like? she asked herself
again, dissatisfied by her own instinctive reaction. She
didn't like Cheryl one bit, and for the stupidest reason:
How could David have fallen in love with a woman so
totally unlike *herself*?

Somehow she'd expected Cheryl to resemble her in
some way; not to be so completely her opposite. After
all, when they'd gone shopping he'd chosen the same
kind of jacket he already had—as if that wasn't the
most idiotic analogy.

But David and Cheryl didn't look as if they matched.
An involuntary sigh of pain escaped her. Now she
didn't just sound stupid, she was starting to sound like
Bea.

"So when's the wedding?" her great-aunt inquired
blithely, skewering Cheryl with a probing look.

"Valentine's Day." Cheryl still looked flustered, and
glanced uncertainly at David.

"Valentine's Day? How romantic." There was an un-
dertone of sarcasm in Bea's voice.

In less than three weeks, he would be married. Suddenly, Lucy couldn't stay a moment longer. Turning

away, she silently slipped out of the room and headed upstairs. She would rather not say goodbye; just let him go, as swiftly as he'd come.

But she hadn't been in the sanctuary of her office very long when a tap at the door made her head jerk around.

David stood in the doorway at the top of the narrow staircase. For a long moment, he just looked at her, his face grim.

"I know this is selfish of me," he said, his voice husky in the quiet attic room, "but I couldn't leave without saying goodbye."

"It's all right, I was just taking the coward's way out...parting being such sweet sorrow, and all that rot." She even managed a smile along with the flippant words, although it made the muscles in her face hurt.

"I feel like I'm leaving behind everything that's dear and familiar...."

She could see the uncertainty, even fear, in his eyes, and who could blame him? How selfish of her to think only of her own pain. She couldn't let him leave without saying goodbye, without reassuring him once more that everything was going to be all right.

Moving toward him, she held out her hand, somehow keeping her smile in place.

"You're going home, David," was all she could say.

He took her hand and lifted it to his lips, their warmth pressing softly against her skin.

"Could I hold you, just one more time?" he murmured against her fingers, his voice husky. "Could you bear to..."

She reached up with her free hand, pulled him down to her, and kissed him gently on the lips.

Even as she drank in the bittersweet pleasure, she knew she had to keep her perspective. It was only his fear of the unknown that made him seek out the comfort of her arms right now. And she refused to feel guilty about that. It was precious little to take before she had to say goodbye forever.

At length he pulled away, and with one last, dark look, he was gone.

She turned to stare blindly out the window as the sound of his footsteps grew fainter and fainter. A moment later, she heard the faraway thunk of the front door closing.

She had no idea how long she stood there.

Suddenly Bea's disgusted voice came from behind her, cutting into her misery. "So, you're just going to stand by and let him leave."

There was no way she wanted her great-aunt to see her face. She shrugged without turning around. "What else can I do? He's going home where he belongs, with the woman he's going to marry."

But Bea moved to stand in front of her. Her mouth tightened to a stubborn crease as her small eyes bored into Lucy. "But he doesn't love her. He loves you."

She started to shake her head in denial, but Bea clamped a hand on her arm, fiercely holding her gaze. "Something happened between you, something magical. You can't deny it."

With a sigh, Lucy drew away. "What happened was probably a predictable response to an unusual circumstance—"

"Lucy, stop it!" Bea rapped out impatiently. "Stop sounding like a textbook and start admitting how you feel. You love him."

"No, I don't." A hand squeezed her heart and she turned away. "Only a fool would allow herself to fall in love with a man who doesn't even know his own name."

And besides, it wasn't love. What had happened between them had sprung from many causes, including sexual attraction. But whatever it was—it wasn't love.

11

"LUCY, CAN YOU COME DOWN? I need you," Bea called up from the bottom of the stairs, breaking into her reverie.

She shook her head to clear the ceaselessly revolving thoughts and slipped on her other earring. "I'll be there in a minute."

With a sigh of resignation, she gave herself one last look in the full-length mirror. It had been so long since she'd worn a dress and put on makeup that she hardly recognized the woman looking back at her.

The ruby velvet dress was one of Bea's thrift-store finds, with a tightly fitted bodice and off-the-shoulder neckline that dipped low in the back. The full skirt brushed her calves above high-heeled black pumps.

She looked nice enough, but the knowledge gave her little pleasure. She didn't really feel like going to the Valentine's Dance, was doing so only because she'd promised Blaine. Besides, anything was better than moping around the house as she'd been doing for the past three weeks.

And she especially needed to get out today, of all days. Had it been a morning wedding? Or were they at this very moment exchanging vows that would bind them to each other for life?

"Lucy, what on earth are you up to, child?"

She sighed. She didn't want to think about that anymore. It was over. It had never even really begun. It was something that happened one night, and now it was in the past.

Resolutely, she walked out of the bedroom and paused at the head of the stairs. Bea stood at the bottom, and the color drained from her great-aunt's face as she caught sight of her.

She put a hand to her chest, looking startled and a little overcome. "Oh, Lucy, you gave me such a turn." There was a catch in her voice. "For a moment, there, I thought I was seeing your grandmother. You look so beautiful, child."

For a moment Bea just stood and gazed up at her, then fished a handkerchief from her pocket and dabbed at her eyes. Heaving a shaky sigh, she straightened her shoulders.

"Come on, Lucy. Hurry." Suddenly she was all bustle again. In a flutter of orange, she turned and disappeared into the living room.

Lucy came slowly down the stairs and followed her to find the room aglow in candlelight. "What's this? What are you doing now?"

Bea sank down cross-legged at the low coffee table, on which was laid out a collection of Mason jars and enameled tins.

"I can't sit by any longer and watch your misery. I've decided it's time to do something about it." She began taking horse chestnuts out of one of the jars and laid out six of them in a row on the table. "I used magic to bring David to us in the first place—I'll use magic to bring him back."

Lucy pressed a hand to her eyes. She had no patience

for this right now. "Have you forgotten it's Valentine's Day today? No amount of magic can change that."

"Lucy, why do you refuse to believe?" her great-aunt demanded severely. "I shouldn't have told you. If there's one thing I don't need, it's your negative vibes. Go away, you unnatural child. I'll do this on my own."

She pulled a skein of red thread from a tin and began tying a strand around one of the horse chestnuts.

"What are you doing?" Lucy asked, in spite of herself.

"Making knots from the red thread of life, to summon your love and capture his heart. It's an old Celtic charm, to be woven at the waning of the moon." Bea spoke abstractedly as she carefully made knots in the thread.

Lucy smiled wryly to herself as a surge of love washed over her. After all, it was because Bea cared about her that she got up to all this mumbo jumbo.

And if there was one thing she'd gotten out of her experience with David, it was some understanding of herself—of the way life had shaped her. Losing her parents had made her afraid of caring about anyone too much—except for Bea, who'd been her lifeline. At this point, she was glad to be able to give back even a fraction of the love and caring Bea had given her. It hit her like a blow that her great-aunt really was getting old. Despite Bea's vigor and love of life, Lucy wouldn't have her forever. When her great-aunt finally— She swallowed hard, unable to bring herself to even think the word. When Bea was no longer around, she would be all alone. Her great-aunt was right. Lucy wouldn't want to be alone. And David was right, too. Cutting herself off from love would ultimately leave her an empty shell. She needed someone with whom she could share her life—someone to grow old with. She had to risk letting herself love, and be loved.

She watched Bea bend her white head intently over the knots, and knew it would make her great-aunt so happy if she found that person. Perhaps Blaine could be that person, if she gave him a chance. Tonight would be the beginning of David's new life, and it would be her new beginning, too. He'd given her something very special—a part of herself. She would always be grateful for that, and cherish the memory of what they'd shared. Suddenly her misery lifted a little, and she was filled with a sincere wish for David to have a happy life. He deserved it.

She walked over to her great-aunt, bent down and planted a kiss on the wrinkled old cheek. "I love you."

But her great-aunt wasn't paying attention. She was busy rummaging in another of the small tins and chanting.

"Oh, Diana, goddess whose arrows never fail, help your daughter, Lucy. Bind her forever with her love...."

She scooped up a handful of something from the tin and flung it at Lucy.

"Magic seed, doubting heart, never let them stay apart..." Bea chanted.

Lucy flinched as the grainy stuff hit her in the face. "What is this?" she asked, brushing the specks from her bare shoulders.

"Fennel, sacred to Diana, goddess of love and the hunt."

"Okay, you've convinced me," Lucy said dryly, and gave Bea an indulgent smile. "How would you like

Blaine Stewart as a great-nephew-in-law?'' she added, trying to sound casual.

Her great-aunt looked at her closely. ''Of course, I've always thought Blaine was a very nice boy....''

The ringing of the doorbell echoed through the house.

Lucy headed for the hall. ''That'll be Blaine now. Don't wait up for me,'' she said over her shoulder.

''Have a good time,'' Bea called after her, but there was an odd, thoughtful note in her voice.

What was wrong now? Why wasn't Bea jumping for joy? Maybe she was just stunned because she'd never thought she would hear those words.

Lucy flung open the door and the breath left her body as if she'd been hit in the stomach. Was this some sort of cruel dream?

''David! What are you doing here?'' She stared up at him, unable to believe her eyes. Her senses leaped, but she quickly reined them in.

There was none of the warmth she'd known in his expression. She met the eyes of a stranger—penetrating, yet guarded.

''Lucy!'' Bea's sharp, admonishing voice cut through her shock.

She realized she was shivering, but she couldn't really feel anything. She felt numb.

''What's the matter with you, girl? Shut that door. You're letting in all the cold.'' Bea had come out into the hall, and the annoyance in her voice turned to pleasure. ''David! You dear boy, you're back. I knew you'd come. Why are you standing on the doorstep? Come in, come in.''

As Lucy stood staring stupidly, Bea moved past her.

She took his arm, dragged him over the threshold and helped him off with his coat—the navy parka he'd bought in town.

Quickly, Lucy moved to shut the door, cutting off the bone-chilling cold. Turning reluctantly, she found him silently watching her, as Bea's expectant glance flew back and forth between them.

There was no sign in his grave face that he was happy to be here. And once again she wondered what had brought him here.

"Lucy, aren't you going to say something to David?"

David? This wasn't David. This was an affluent stranger in casual but expensive clothes, with an impenetrable guard around him. This wasn't the man she'd come to know, the man she'd held in her arms, the man she'd confided in.

"This is quite a surprise. What are you doing here?" She tried to keep her tone conversational and light.

"I was on my way up north to go skiing, and I couldn't resist stopping in—"

He had stopped in on his way to his honeymoon? Was this some kind of joke? Maybe there really was something to Bea's spells; but she was obviously screwing up in some vital way.

"But I see I've caught you at a bad time," he continued. "You're obviously going out."

His glance ran over her bare shoulders above the ruby velvet and took in the full skirt floating over layers of petticoats. But she couldn't tell if he liked what he saw.

"Bad time!" Bea exclaimed. "As if there could be a bad time to see you. This is a wonderful surprise, but let's not hang around here—it's too chilly. Come on in by the fire."

Lucy remained hovering by the door. Blaine would be here any moment.

Bea bustled off down the hall toward the back parlor. Without turning, she said sharply, "You, too, Lucy."

Did her great-aunt have eyes in the back of her head?

As he turned to follow Bea, David's brows lifted a little in commiseration. It was the first sign of real communication she'd seen, but nothing to get excited about.

"Is Cheryl waiting in the car?" It wouldn't hurt to remind Bea that David was a married man now. "Perhaps she'd like to come in, too."

"No, she's not," he said in that bland stranger's voice.

Lucy thanked God he must have dropped her at the lodge first. As it was, she should be congratulating him on his marriage, but she couldn't bring herself to do it. So much for all that happiness she'd been wishing him a little while ago.

Feeling like a miserable hypocrite, she followed Bea and David. If only Blaine would just hurry up and get here. All she wanted right now was to escape.

Bea sat on the love seat, patting the cushion next to her. David sank down beside her, while Lucy perched on the edge of the armchair by the door.

"Now, what's been happening?" Bea began confidentially. "Tell us everything."

"That's exactly why I'm here—to tell you everything. I finally got my memory back, and I wanted to come and let you both know something about the man you harbored from the storm." He looked over at Lucy. "But I think I should have called first."

"Nonsense. You're part of the family. There's no need to stand on ceremony," Bea said decisively.

Her great-aunt's words should have put him at ease, but now Lucy sensed even more tension under that impassive mask. Where was the strong and tender lover with whom she'd shared an intensity of passion unlike anything she'd never known before?

"Well, don't keep us in suspense. Tell us everything! What made your memory return?" Bea demanded.

He shrugged. "It wasn't anything dramatic. It just happened." An odd look crossed his face. "You'll be glad to know you didn't have a madman on your hands, after all. By the way, was that guy in Witchwood really an escaped lunatic? Did you find out?" He smiled now, but the tension was still there.

"Yes, and yes," Bea said confidentially. "As you can imagine, Blaine's confirmation was a huge relief to me. I was starting to feel quite responsible."

He chuckled as Bea went on. "But enough about lunatics in doughnut shops. What about you, dear boy?"

He shook his head. "I'm nothing too dangerous— just a humble writer, scratching out a living."

"A writer!" Her eyes sparkled. "Oh, that's very exciting, isn't it, Lucy?"

"Yes, very interesting," she said dully. Somehow it seemed to fit: that penetrating way he had of watching the world around him, his interest in and sympathy for people.

Bea gave her an impatient look before her gaze flashed back to David. "What do you write?"

"Before the accident I was working on a book about

my experiences in Central America. I used to be a journalist. Covered quite a few hot spots."

That explained the memories of the jungle. "Is that how you got that bullet wound?" She was surprised to hear her own voice. She hadn't felt capable of making small talk.

He turned to her with that same dead, careful look. "Yes." Then, as if realizing he had to offer more of an explanation, he added offhandedly, "I was in the wrong place at the wrong time. But I don't do that anymore."

He was becoming more of a stranger to her with each passing moment.

The sound of the doorbell suddenly echoed through the house again.

Lucy jumped to her feet and rushed out. Thank God it was Blaine standing on the threshold. She was about to yell out a hurried goodbye when Bea called from the parlor.

"Is that Blaine? Why don't you bring him in and introduce him to David?"

Blaine had already stepped through the door and heard Bea's invitation, leaving Lucy with no choice but to lead him down the hall.

As they walked through the French doors to the back parlor, David got to his feet.

"No need for introductions, Bea," Blaine said in his easygoing manner. "David and I have already met."

"Yes. Blaine was nice enough to come down and help us dig out the car." David reached out and shook the other man's hand.

"Oh, I see." Bea looked from one to the other speculatively.

"We'd better get going," Lucy said to Blaine. She just couldn't bear to stay here a moment longer. Somehow she met David's eyes and forced a smile to her lips. "It was good to see you again. I'm glad everything is working out." She turned to her great-aunt. "Don't wait up for me, Bea. We'll probably be late."

Giving her great-aunt a kiss on the cheek and David a tight smile, she spun on her heel and hurried from the room. Grabbing her coat from the closet, she flung it on and stepped through the door that Blaine was holding open for her.

The cold air hit her face. After the blizzards had passed, there'd been no more snow, but a deep freeze had set in.

It was a clear night. The moon was ablaze, outshining the stars. Every so often little gusts of wind whisked across the snow, causing glittering showers of flakes. It was a gloriously beautiful night—that touched her not at all.

The door clicked shut behind Blaine. He took her arm, walked her down the steps and toward his car.

Feeling numb and desolate, she barely looked at the Mercedes parked next to it. All she could think about was that by the time she got back, David would be gone. Maybe then she could finally get on with her life again.

THE DOOR BANGED SHUT and silence descended. David turned to find Bea giving him a shrewd, direct look.

"Aren't you going to do anything?" she asked sharply. "She'll marry Blaine, you know."

A fist of pain squeezed his chest. "When?"

She tutted impatiently. "It hasn't gotten that far yet.

But she wants to please me, and Blaine's a good man. And she'll do it, too, unless you do something about it."

"What can I do? It's too late now."

Lucy didn't want him, anyway. She seemed withdrawn and so ill at ease. The woman who'd made love to him with such fire and passion was gone. Obviously she'd thought he was out of her life; saw him as just another temporary and uncomplicated lover who'd had the bad judgment to return.

A cold, dark void filled his chest. Suddenly, he didn't feel like going skiing anymore.

12

AS THEY PULLED OUT of the driveway onto the snowy highway, Lucy stared blindly out the car window. The light from the full moon gilded the pines and made the snow-covered fields glitter. So beautiful. But right now, she didn't care.

Why had he come? Why couldn't he have just called? Seeing him again had driven it home with piercing certainty: What she felt for him was, indeed, love.

Dragging in a deep breath, she closed her eyes for a moment. She could, and would get a grip on herself. But she'd been right to fear love, to fear the pain it brought with it.

She just had to remember that this would pass. Time would heal her. Resolutely, she turned to Blaine.

He glanced over at her and smiled. "You look very beautiful tonight, Lucy."

"Thank you, Blaine. You look very nice, too." And he did. Under a heavy tweed topcoat he was wearing a navy suit that accentuated his blond good looks.

Yes, he was definitely terrific husband material. He had everything she was looking for. Although she wasn't in love with him, she felt great affection and respect for Blaine. He was a very good man. And she could be a very good wife.

There was no reason they couldn't have a satisfying relationship, guided by rational thought rather than by uncontrollable emotions. The knowledge comforted her and made her even more confident in her decision. She wasn't making a mistake by choosing him.

Just as important, Bea liked Blaine, too. She thought he was a nice, steady young man, and their marriage would give her peace and happiness in her remaining years.

Lucy suddenly realized they had reached the middle of town and turned down Empress Avenue. Up ahead, the old Atkinson mansion was ablaze with lights that gleamed off the snow.

Blaine let her out at the front door and drove off to park the car. Lucy hurried into the foyer of the grand old house that had been donated to the town for use as a community center.

As people streamed in, checking their coats and boots at the door, many called out greetings and several stopped to ask after Bea. But when Blaine finally joined her, she couldn't remember a single face or a word of conversation.

She felt numb. But that was only natural. After all, this was a turning point in her life. It wasn't every day she decided to get married.

Blaine escorted her into the large main hall, which was paneled in carved oak and had three chandeliers hanging from the high ceiling. The Atkinsons had been timber barons and had spared no expense when building this turreted, gabled mansion.

As she and Blaine walked in, the chandeliers dimmed and a mirrored ball began to twirl, throwing out a million points of reflected light. The hall was full already, with people seated at tables around the dance floor. The theme this year was the big-band era. And right on cue, the orchestra began to play, "In the Mood."

Blaine held out his hand and smiled down at her. "Let's go show them how it's done," he said.

Lucy chuckled. "Yes, let's."

They joined the other dancers crowding the floor. What Blaine lacked in skill, he made up for in energy, and Lucy could only do her best to keep up. But by the end of the jitterbug à la Blaine, she was clinging for dear life, breathless and laughing.

Blaine was laughing, too.

The band struck up something slow and mellow, and they began moving in a more sedate rhythm.

After a few moments, he smiled down at her. "Got your breath back?"

"Oh, yes. I love to dance." But she felt too miserable to hold his keen glance. She turned her head to watch the other couples on the floor.

"Look, Lucy..." His voice softened, and his hand squeezed hers a little tighter, comfortingly. "You don't have to tell me what's wrong if you don't want to. But is there anything I can do to help?"

His kindness made her feel even worse. But she just looked up at him and smiled. "You've already helped by bringing me here. It's been a long winter."

He had an understanding look in his eyes. "That's for sure. You know that fella we picked up in Witchwood? Turned out he'd run away from a group home. He had a whole list of problems, but they said what pushed him over the edge was what they called 'light deprivation.'" He shook his head. "Not enough sunlight can make you crazy, and we haven't seen much of that in the past few months."

Maybe that was the key to her recent inexplicable behavior: light deprivation. Any other man in that situation would probably have had the same effect on her.

But now she was getting back to her normal routine; she was no longer snowbound. No doubt these feelings would fall away. Seeing David tonight had been a shock, but only because his appearance had been so unexpected. She would be over it soon.

But suddenly she had the overwhelming urge to go home before it was too late.

Too late! For what? It was already too late. It was all over. He was married. Besides, the man she had known bore no resemblance to the stranger she'd met this evening. And yet she felt a stab of regret for having left so quickly. She should at least have talked to him. Instead she'd run, like a rat leaving a burning ship. Because she was afraid that if she'd stayed, she would have betrayed her feelings.

Blaine stopped moving and seemed to stiffen a little.

"Can I cut in?"

The shock of hearing the familiar husky voice behind her made her heart stop beating for a moment. If she hadn't been in Blaine's arms, she might actually have sunk to the floor.

She turned slowly to see Bea and David standing behind her. He was looking down at her with an absolutely unreadable expression.

"What are you doing here?" Lucy demanded weakly.

"I had a hankering to go to the ball, so I asked Prince Charming to bring me," Bea said forthrightly, looking breathtaking in purple satin.

But Lucy could barely concentrate on her great-aunt; she was much too aware of David.

"Will you dance with me?" His voice was hard, intense.

She should say no. Why prolong the agony?

"Please?" he added. "I'd like to talk to you." She could see the tension glittering in his eyes.

If this was about guilt, then she should let him talk and get it off his conscience.

She turned to Blaine. He smiled understandingly. "Go ahead." Then he turned to her great-aunt with an endearing grin. "Miss Bea, would you care to dance?"

"I thought you'd never ask." Bea allowed him to sweep her off to the opening strains of "Moonlight Serenade."

Lucy remained frozen in place. David stepped closer, put an arm around her waist and took her hand.

The sudden, intoxicating feel of his body pressed against hers, the scent of him, filled her head and sent waves of need flooding through her.

Finally, she could bring herself to look above his chin. She raised her eyes and stared into his brilliantly blue ones. He was gazing down at her with an enigmatic, veiled expression.

"What are you doing here, anyway?" Her voice sounded annoyingly thin.

"I wanted to see you before I left."

"It really wasn't necessary. Everything's fine. I'm fine." She took a deep breath. Here was her chance to wish him all that happiness she'd so sincerely desired. "I haven't congratulated you on your marriage yet."

"We need to find a place to talk," David said abruptly, as he stopped dancing and looked around impatiently.

Taking her hand, he drew her out of the main hall into the adjoining glass-roofed conservatory. Feeling confused, she let herself be led. He drew her into a shadowy corner and they sank down onto a bench concealed behind a bank of tall, potted palms.

For a long moment, he just frowned at her. She sat numbly, waiting for him to speak.

"When I met Cheryl," he began slowly—and she felt her heart sink; she didn't want to hear about Cheryl. "I'd just recovered from this bullet I took in the shoulder. That is, I had recovered physically, but I wasn't human anymore."

Her tension eased a little, and she was curious. "What do you mean, you weren't human anymore?"

He hesitated, then drew in a deep breath. "I told you I was a journalist. I worked for one of the wire services, and they sent me all over the world, wherever people were shooting at each other."

She shuddered at the thought of him being in constant danger.

He sighed heavily. "My last assignment was in Colombia. I'd been there for a while and had worked quite closely with a local journalist. Carlos and I were good friends. He helped me set up a meeting with one of the major guerilla leaders at a jungle village."

"Your dream about the jungle," she said.

"Exactly." He nodded. "We'd just walked into the village—a peaceful, quiet sort of place—and suddenly all hell broke loose. One moment I was standing there, the next moment I felt like my shoulder was on fire. I fell to the ground, crawled under some bushes and passed out. When I came to, everyone in the village lay dead, including my friend Carlos. I was the only survivor." His voice remained even and dispassionate, but she could sense his despair.

"Oh, David, I'm so sorry." Sick with horror, she reached out and clutched his arm.

"When I got back to Bogotá, I got on the first plane and came home for good."

She shuddered. "Thank God you made it out of that place alive."

He heaved another sigh. "I'm not so sure I did. Pretty soon after I got home, I realized that part of me had died that day. I couldn't feel anything anymore."

"But that's understandable. For so long, you'd just been a helpless observer of all that death and misery. Anyone would burn out."

"That's what I told myself. Anyway, then I met Cheryl."

She felt an acute pang of jealousy at hearing the other woman's name and fought to quell it.

He sighed. "She was so removed from all of that. She didn't watch the news, didn't even read the papers. She was an escape for me. Being with her kept all that ugliness at bay. I was grateful, and thought I'd gotten back some semblance of normalcy. But that wasn't true. I was still dead inside. And then came the accident.

"When I came to, I didn't remember anything about myself, but I could feel again. The numbness had gone, although I didn't know it at the time."

She couldn't help wondering if that had something to do with her. No, it was probably just the amnesia.

"When I went back with Cheryl, I realized that until my memory returned, I couldn't bring myself to take such an irrevocable step as marriage. I asked Cheryl to give me more time."

"Because of what happened when you were here?"

"No." He shook his head briefly. "Because of what I didn't feel for Cheryl."

Her heart was pounding painfully against her ribs, and she could hardly speak. "I don't understand." Her voice emerged a husky croak.

"I was expecting her to be angry and disappointed, but she wasn't. In fact, she confessed to me that neither of us was getting married for the right reason. Needless to say I was shocked. And then she explained what had happened the night of my accident. That's when my memory all came flooding back."

"What happened?" she asked, breathlessly eager.

"I found her with another man, an old friend of mine."

"Oh, David. That must have been so painful for you."

But his voice was still quite unemotional as he went on. "That's just it—it wasn't. It made me realize that I couldn't love Cheryl, and I knew she didn't love me.

She loved Bill. And as soon as he gets his divorce, they'll be getting married."

"So... You didn't get married today?" Hadn't he just been telling her that? It had taken a while to sink into her disbelieving brain.

He hesitated for a moment, then gave her a wry smile. "It's in very bad taste to marry one woman when you're in love with another."

She stared up at him in amazement, then determinedly reeled in her racing thoughts. "You don't have to do this out of any sense of chivalry—"

"Chivalry!" He looked stunned.

There was a long pause. She heard the music start up again.

"Don't marry him."

His quiet, grim words made her heart jump in her chest. "What? Don't marry who?"

The muscles of his face tightened. "Bea said you'd probably marry Blaine."

"Oh," she gasped, hardly able to catch her breath, "she did, did she!"

"Yes. She said you'd probably marry him to make a foolish old lady happy. Is that true?"

"It would make her happy," she said evasively.

"Don't make that decision yet." His voice was impassioned.

"Why not?"

"Because I want you to give me a chance."

If this was a dream, she didn't want to be woken up. She still felt reluctant to believe that anything this miraculous could be true.

"Lucy, I love you. I've never felt this way for any other woman before."

She opened her mouth to speak, but he didn't give her the chance.

"Never," he repeated softly but emphatically.

The music had stopped in the other room, but she hardly cared.

"Would you consider marrying me for the same reasons you were going to marry Blaine?"

"No, I can't do that." Her heart was singing with happiness.

"Why not?"

"Because I love you. I wouldn't be doing it for the same reason at all—"

Her words were cut off precipitously by his mouth covering hers. Her lips clung to him; her tongue met his in a famished kiss.

He drew away. "Are you sure? I know how you feel about emotional dependence."

"I never realized how essential love was to life, to happiness. Now that I've found it, I can't imagine living without it."

"You won't have to live without it. Not as long as there's breath in my body," he murmured fervently.

She tried to contain the soaring happiness that threatened to overwhelm her, tried to bring her mind back to practical considerations. "But how would we manage? You in Toronto, me up here."

He lifted her hand to his lips. His touch sent a warm tingle up her arm to fill her entire body. "I was thinking of staying on. I believe there are some good B and

B's around these parts." His mouth curved in a small, teasing smile.

"You'd do that for me?"

"That, and a whole lot more."

"Can this be real?" She felt the need once again to be the voice of reason. "We only had a few days."

"Maybe. But for me, it took only a few hours."

"For me, seconds," she said, slightly dazed by her growing elation. "One moment, actually. The moment I first saw you—"

Once again, she didn't have a chance to finish her sentence before his mouth covered hers.

The music stopped again, making her aware of where they were. No one could see them, but there were people just on the other side of the palms behind the bench where they sat.

Reluctantly, she ended the kiss. He relinquished her lips with a sigh of frustration. But she pushed him firmly away.

"Not here," she said, her voice a shaky whisper.

"Then let's go home," he groaned, and nuzzled her jawline.

All she had to do was turn her head. She *wanted* to turn her head and lose herself in another delirious kiss, but she fought the temptation.

"I love you more than I ever thought it was possible to love. It's so..." He shook his head. "I've always made my living with words, but now, when I need them most, I don't know how to express myself. I never knew it could be like this."

She saw love, hunger and tenderness in his eyes—a

wild tangle of emotions that made her heart expand in her chest and filled her with joy.

"I understand now how much my mother must have loved my father. Because all I want is to be with you, wherever you are."

With David's hand in hers, she walked back into the ballroom, feeling as if she glowed from the inside out. How was it possible to feel so much happiness?

She saw Blaine through the crowd, dancing with a pretty young woman she didn't recognize. He caught her eye, giving her a wink and a smile. Behind the smile she saw an acceptance that relieved her guilt a little.

At that moment, Bea materialized in front of them. "Well?" She had an eager twinkle in her eyes. "Do you have some news for me?"

"I guess I don't have to worry about getting your permission to marry your niece," David said with a smile.

"Took you long enough, dear boy. Although I knew from the very start it would happen."

Lucy grinned. Trust Bea to be so blasé. "It wasn't exactly a foregone conclusion, but I have to admit it's all quite unbelievable."

"Just as if someone cast a spell on us." David looked at Bea with a mischievous gleam in his eye.

"You don't believe in hocus-pocus, do you?" she asked coyly.

"No, but I thought you did," Lucy said, giving her great-aunt an arch look.

Bea smirked. "Well, it just goes to show, the power of suggestion is a wonderful thing. Don't you agree?

When David showed such impeccable timing with his arrival, I realized I couldn't let a godsend go to waste. Especially when I saw the way you two looked at each other. The air positively sizzled when you were in the room together. Now, if that isn't supernatural, what is?''

"You're right," Lucy said, looking at the man by her side. "I do believe in magic, after all."

David's eyes glowed with heady warmth as they met hers. He pulled her into his arms as the music swelled again to the familiar, poignant strains of "Stardust." His touch made her feel complete as he held her close and a million stars whirled around them.

The beginning of a huge adventure stretched before her—a future she was eager to embrace, not hide from. Love had come when she'd least expected it, and had changed her life.

Standing on tiptoe, she whispered into David's ear: "The magic is love."

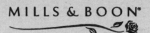

This month's irresistible novels from

Temptation®

ROARKE: THE ADVENTURER by JoAnn Ross

New Orleans Lovers

Shaken by an attempt on his life, journalist Roarke O'Malley returned home. But he was thrown into more danger when beautiful Daria Shea turned to him for help. Without her memory, she had no idea who was trying to hurt her or why... And as they investigated together, the sultry days turned into hot, passionate nights...

NOT THIS GAL! by Glenda Sanders

Brides on the Run

Keeley Owens was in a tacky Las Vegas wedding chapel, about to marry her drunken boyfriend, when she realized it would be a fate worse than death. So she stalked off into the desert—only to be rescued by a gorgeous stranger. He wined her, dined her and loved her all night long. But Keeley had only just left one groom at the altar...

ONE ENCHANTED NIGHT by Debra Carroll

It Happened One Night

The man Lucy Weston found on her doorstep was half-dead from the winter storm outside. She kept him alive with the warmth of her body, and reacted to him as she never had to any man. He was a strong, sensual lover. But he had no idea who he was...

ONE HOT SUMMER by Suzanne Scott

Jillian Sanderson had just inherited half an inn—but the other half was a problem. Because that half belonged to sexy-as-sin Kit Malone...and the fever that raged between them was uncontrollable. Would Kit stay around if they could make those hot summer nights last forever?

MARY LYNN BAXTER

Raw Heat

Successful broadcast journalist Juliana Reed is caught
in a web of corruption, blackmail and murder. Texas
Ranger, Gates O'Brien—her ex-husband—is the only
person she can turn to. Both know that getting out
alive is just the beginning...

*"Baxter's writing...strikes every chord within
the female spirit."*
—Bestselling author Sandra Brown

MIRA®

1-55166-394-5
AVAILABLE FROM APRIL 1998

NORA ROBERTS

Hot Ice

She had the cash and the connections. He knew
the whereabouts of a fabulous hidden fortune. It
was a business proposition, pure and simple.
Now all they needed to do was stay one step
ahead of their murderous rivals.

*"...her stories have fuelled the dreams of
25 million readers"*—Entertainment Weekly

1-55166-395-3
AVAILABLE FROM APRIL 1998

INTERNATIONAL BESTSELLING AUTHOR

Karen Young

Good Girls

When they were good...

Jack Sullivan is an ambitious and painful presence in
the lives of three prominent Mississippi women.
He made Suzanne a prisoner of violent memories,
used Taylor as a lonely trophy wife and drove
Annie's mother to suicide. When Jack is murdered,
each wonders who finally pulled the trigger...

"Karen Young is a spellbinding storyteller."
—Romantic Times

MIRA®

1-55166-306-6
AVAILABLE FROM MAY 1998

DANCE FEVER

How would you like to win a year's supply of Mills & Boon®
books? Well you can and they're FREE! Simply complete the
competition below and send it to us by 31st October 1998.
The first five correct entries picked after the closing date will
each win a year's subscription to the Mills & Boon series of
their choice. What could be easier?

OBLARMOL
AMBUR
RTOXTFO
RASQUE
GANCO

KOPLA
OOOOMTLCIN
MALOENCF
SITWT
LASSA

EVJI
TAZLW
ACHACH
SCDIO
MAABS

G	R	I	H	C	H	A	R	J	T	O	N
O	P	A	R	L	H	U	B	P	I	B	W
M	O	O	R	L	L	A	B	M	C	V	H
B	L	D	I	O	O	K	C	L	U	P	E
R	K	U	B	N	C	R	Q	H	V	R	Z
S	A	N	I	O	O	N	G	W	A	S	V
T	S	I	N	R	M	G	E	U	B	G	H
W	L	G	H	S	O	R	Q	M	M	B	L
I	A	P	N	O	T	S	L	R	A	H	C
S	S	L	U	K	I	A	S	F	S	L	S
T	O	R	T	X	O	F	O	X	T	R	F
G	U	I	P	Z	N	D	I	S	C	O	Q

D8C

Please turn over for details of how to enter ⇨

HOW TO ENTER

There is a list of fifteen mixed up words overleaf, all of which when unscrambled spell popular dances. When you have unscrambled each word, you will find them hidden in the grid. They may appear forwards, backwards or diagonally. As you find each one, draw a line through it. Find all fifteen and fill in the coupon below then pop this page into an envelope and post it today. Don't forget you could win a year's supply of Mills & Boon® books—you don't even need to pay for a stamp!

Mills & Boon Dance Fever Competition
FREEPOST CN81, Croydon, Surrey, CR9 3WZ
EIRE readers send competition to PO Box 4546, Dublin 24.

Please tick the series you would like to receive if you are one of the lucky winners

Presents™ ❏   Enchanted™ ❏   Medical Romance™ ❏
Historical Romance™ ❏   Temptation® ❏

Are you a Reader Service™ subscriber?   Yes ❏   No ❏

Ms/Mrs/Miss/Mr ....Intials ....
(BLOCK CAPITALS PLEASE)

Surname...

Address ....

....

....Postcode...........................

(I am over 18 years of age)   D8C

Closing date for entries is 31st October 1998.
One application per household. Competition open to residents of the UK and Ireland only. You may be mailed with offers from other reputable companies as a result of this application. If you would prefer not to receive such offers, please tick this box.   ❏

Mills & Boon is a registered trademark of
Harlequin Mills & Boon Ltd.